It's
no
Longer
a
Dream!

By the same author

In Course of True Love!

It's no Longer a Dream!

Sanjeev Ranjan

Srishti
PUBLISHERS & DISTRIBUTORS

SRISHTI PUBLISHERS & DISTRIBUTORS
N-16, C. R. Park
New Delhi 110 019
editorial@srishtipublishers.com

First published by
Srishti Publishers & Distributors in 2014

Typeset by Eshu Graphic

To Papa, of course for everything

Contents

Acknowledgements

Papa, Mummy, Bhabhi, Sis, and my big brother – thank you all for your unconditional support. Papa, thank you for your positive nod over whatever I wanted to do in my life.

This book happened because of two persons without whom it would have been tough to finish the book Rakesh Kumar and Gaurav Deka – my friends, confidants and well-wishers. Someone had told me a few years back, "Don't worry! You just start your journey and you will meet someone to help you and walk with you along the journey."

Gaurav, truly glad to meet you! Rakesh, thanks for helping me in every possible way, without asking any questions, and understanding me. It's rare to find a friend like you. Thank you both for tolerating my eccentricities, bearing my frustrations, listening to my useless chatter for hours without interrupting me when things looked too dark. Special thanks for reading the drafts over and over again, without getting bugged and giving me invaluable suggestions.

Before I pay my gratitude to anyone else, I would like to thank my dear and lovely readers who bought my first book, read it and took the pain to connect with me. Thank you so much. It's your love and affection that motivated me to pen down this one.

I also thank Surabhi Priyadarshini for listening to my unnecessary details about books and laughing on my poor jokes over phone, in spite of your tight schedule, that too without getting irritated. Thank you so much for being in my life, and supporting me during this journey.

Nachiket, for being my early mentor and friend, for supporting during my rough days in college, for listening to several other things that hardly interested you. I am indebted to you for life.

Rishabh, for showing confidence in me and encouraging me all the time. You words: "Sanjeev, I know you can do it" always motivated me.

Harsha Prerna, Udita Pal, Ayushee Ghosal and Divya Sharma, I am grateful for your support, taking out time to read my drafts and giving me suggestions. Harsha and Udita: special thanks for making me feel like I belong to Bokaro and supporting me everywhere.

Srishti Publishers, for helping me at every stage of publishing, guiding me, sorting out my queries, and the careful, wise and razor-sharp editing. Thanks to the entire Sristhi team for helping me throughout the process.

Sunil, you are one amazing designer Thanks a lot for listening to the minute details and implementing on the cover design. Special thanks for giving your best and for designing such a brilliant and beautiful design.

Last of all, my deepest and most sincere thanks to all those who remained connected to me all the time, and showed faith in me.

Prologue

Something was different that day. It was as if the air itself was singing a slow melody and wooing my soul. I stopped walking. I closed my eyes, trying to feel it… breathe it all in. This was all new… and so breathtakingly beautiful. Trees I saw every day suddenly seemed greener; the sky was a richer blue than ever before. The scent of spring was in the wind. I had walked down this path every day of my life, but I had never found it so beautiful before.

My mind flew back to those countless desolate walks. I remembered the heaviness of my heart, the claustrophobia that held a deathly grip on my life. I had come to terms with a lot in the past few days; I was no longer the same man.

I opened my eyes and gazed at the large mansion that lay nestled in the landscaped gardens at the end of the path. I walked towards the house I was born in.

As I neared the gate, the watchman stared at me as if he were seeing a ghost.

"Sa'ab!" he exclaimed, and then he ran away from me towards the dining hall instead of opening the gate for me. *Saab ji aa gaye! Saab ji aa gaye!*

The man of the house had arrived. Having run almost halfway down the driveway, he remembered that I was still waiting. He rushed back and apologized profusely before opening the gate and letting me in. The rest of the staff had come out running by now. They all were staring at me.

"What? I'm not a ghost." The words dropped out of my mouth and their jubilant smiles brought a reluctant smile to my own face.

"Saab ji, where've you been? We were all so worried for you. Going away like that without telling us…"

I didn't want to answer their questions yet. The best I could do was set them all to work, make them busy. I gave instructions for hot tea and *pakodas.*

They left reluctantly. Kaka, my valet (isn't it funny we still have them in this day and age), remained.

He was old; he was persistent; he was fiercely protective of me. He wouldn't leave without answers.

I walked to my room, opened the door, and sat down on the sofa.

"It's good to be back," I said, by way of conversation.

"Where *have* you been, Akshat baba? We've been really worried for you. Do you know… Naina ji used to come here every day. She waited and waited… for just one call. She kept trying to call you, but couldn't reach you… All this while, we were so worried!"

"Oh, I was just… you know… here and there. I'd sent an e-mail to dad about where I was."

"Bade saab never told us anything."

"I'm back now, so don't worry."

"Ok, Akshat baba. I'll go get something for you to eat."

He still looked worried as he turned to go.

I'd asked him to stop calling me 'baba', but dear man that

he was, refused to acknowledge that you only address kids like that. I had grown up more in the past week than I had in past years. I placed a hand on his shoulder as he started toward the door.

"Kaka… I can't tell you how grateful I am for all the love you and the rest of our staff have given me. I don't know if I deserve it, but I do appreciate it a lot. And you make my house… a home for me."

He was stunned. He turned to look at me, his eyes wide. I'd never bothered to acknowledge this before. As he stepped out the door, I noticed that some of the others had also heard what I'd said. They were embarrassed. Strangely though, I wasn't. I smiled and returned to my sofa.

My gaze went to the red diary I had left on my desk.

I must have stood for a full minute, staring at it as my mind tried to cope with the sudden storm of thoughts and memories that assailed me. There was much writing to be done… many promises to be kept…

I decided to take a shower before I got down to business.

As I dried my hair after the shower, still looking at my diary and wondering how I was going to put into words my experiences of the past week, I suddenly realized that I hadn't seen my cell phone all this while.

It lay quiet on the desk. I picked it up and pressed the button that would bring it back to life. Alas, it stayed lifeless… drained of battery perhaps. I plugged in the charger and waited for it to power back on.

After a minute, what seemed like a thousand beeps began announcing the messages and missed calls. I waited for the beeps to stop. The screen showed 239 missed calls and 127 messages. I sighed. They would all have to wait.

I sat down at my desk and opened my diary, carefully flipping every page till I arrived at March 27, 2012. Today. And I began writing…

I am in love. When did that happen?

I couldn't get past those two sentences.

PART 1

1

Of Remembrances and Hope

I couldn't get past those two sentences. I gathered myself for a moment and started writing yet again.

I am in love. When did that happen?

How could it have happened? I, Akshat, am in love? Difficult to believe, even for me… but it's true.

Is it possible that I could have finally changed my idea about love? I had been asking myself this for the last two years but hadn't found an answer, until the past seven days. The days that had changed everything. I had been pushed beyond the boundaries of life, had realized things that I had never been ready to understand.

I pondered over these questions alone in my room, sitting at the window, watching the empty street. In the humdrum of such banality, everything seemed out of focus. It brought out mixed feelings. First, a pain, then the relief of a warm breeze.

I walked up to the window and looked up at the sky. It was a riot of colours. A deep indigo fading into blue, splashed with the bright yellow and orange of the setting sun. There was pleasant warmth in the air though it was not yet summer. It was a curious mix, cool and yet warm. As usual, I didn't know where my parents were, and I didn't care asking anyone about them.

As the sky turned red and the sun became distant, the darkness in my room started to grow. A whirlpool of questions was flooding my mind, the answers to which were perhaps in an unknown oblivion. Daylight eventually left, and made way for the night. I kept staring at the lamp at the centre of my desk.

There was definitely a change, and searching for reasons would make me more confused. I stopped and started pondering over what had happened in the last seven days and watched the twilight sky; to me, its darkness reflected my empty soul.

The thought sent a strange tightness to my chest, and a tear rolled down my eye. Startled, I crushed the tear to nothingness between my fingers. I couldn't explain the feelings brewing in my heart. I was expectant, yet calm; torn, yet whole.

I had never considered myself a sentimental person, and if you ask my friends, they would agree with me. Not all of them though: ask Naina, Naina Malhotra – a secret lover that I hadn't recognized in the face of a friend. I came to know about her feelings a year ago, about thoughts she never revealed. If you would ask her this, she would definitely agree. Why wouldn't she? I was aware of the ways I was hurting her, so many times, even at the cost of being called an "insensitive beast". And yet, I continued. I never lost myself in films and songs. That's true; I never indulged in nonsensical things. I hated such things to the core. But that was because of another truth: I never understood emotions; I hated them too.

But today was something different. Deep emotion was flowing out of me and tears kept rolling down.

Until last week, I had not realized the meaning of love.

I didn't notice when someone knocked at the door.

"Baba," he said in a submissive tone and waited for me to reply. When I didn't, he called for me again.

"Akshat baba!"

I was looking outside, trying to calm down the myriads things moving inside my mind. I wiped away the remnants of tears from my eyes. I knew Kaka would know I had been crying so I asked back in a feeble tone, "Umm... What did you say just now?"

"Your room is so dark; even the light is switched off. Were you sleeping, baba?" he asked, entering the room.

"No, it is just..," I started, but found this an inappropriate question. "And is that why you came to my room? To ask me whether I keep my lights switched on or off?"

"No. I came to your room because of a phone call."

"A phone call? Who is it?" I asked politely. By then, he had switched on the light and the room was bright again.

"I got a call from Naina ma'am's place, asking whether you are home or not. They told me that it's her birthday today and that she is waiting for you."

On hearing his words, I checked my watch for the date and remembered, "Oh God! It's her birthday. It's Naina's birthday! How could I forget?"

"So... well, she wants you to go over like you always do. She said she won't cut the cake until she meets you... but if you're not up to it, I'll tell her you are unwell."

"No Kaka. I must go. I will."

"Ok then, baba. I will tell the driver."

He left.

Year after year, Naina had celebrated her birthday with me. She would wait for me and would cut the cake only when I was there, however long it may take. She would give the third piece of cake to me – the first two pieces were for her parents. She would wait with the piece of cake in her hands until I would give her my gift, and then she would fill my mouth. This was quickly followed by her opening up the gift-wrapping in childlike haste.

This year I had something special for her. I opened the cupboard, took out the two packets, and kept them on the table. I was filled with trepidation. And yet, I was hopeful. I guess that about sums up the state of my mind that day – torn into two.

I took a bath and then stood confused before my wardrobe, unable to find anything suitable for the occasion. This had never happened before. Though nothing seemed good enough, I dressed myself in *kurta* and dabbed myself with the perfume that Naina had gifted. As I was about to leave for her place, it began raining, with gentle tapping sounds. I looked at the sky and hoped that it won't last long.

When I reached her house, I saw that it was ablaze with glittering lights. And why not: Naina was the apple of her parents' eye. They wouldn't spare any expense to give her joy.

I knew the door was open, but still knocked and entered into the main hall. Soft, romantic music was playing. The room was filled with lots of people, and most of them were young. I guessed they might be Naina's father's colleagues. Looking at them, I felt embarrassed: the men were dressed in suits and ladies in expensive, well-fitted attire, evening gowns.

It was then that I suddenly realized that Naina was nowhere to be seen. I felt uncomfortable and left out, even as her mother asked me to take a seat.

Few minutes passed, and from the other door, Naina entered the main hall. When I saw her piercing green eyes look straight at me, I couldn't help suppress a smile. A pleasant, joyful smile. Her lips were coloured red with lipstick, and her cheeks glowed under the light of the chandelier. The smile was of course radiant. She moved towards her friends, politely thanking them for coming, accepting their gifts. At last, she came towards me, and when she looked at me, I dropped my eyelids. But after a few seconds, when I raised my eyes, I found her still looking at me. Naturally, her face was suffused with pink whenever she saw me. I willed myself to smile, but I could only manage a grimace. My heart was thudding so hard, I wondered irrationally if she could hear it above the beats of the songs playing in the background.

I had never found her so beautiful. I just looked around, and a ray of astonishment drew itself on both of our faces with an involuntarily expression of pleasure.

"You are beautiful."

Why did I blurt that out? No, that's okay. I should be honest with my feelings.

She *was* beautiful.

She hurried towards me. She refused to let her eyes stray from mine even for a moment, and this filled my heart with a joy I can hardly describe. In seconds, she was before me.

"Happy birthday! Many many happy returns of the day, Naina," I wished her. My eyes were pleading a silent apology.

She was so surprised to see me, I think, that she didn't say a word. She just looked at me and her eyes began to mist over.

"It's your birthday. Now cheer up, I'm here," I smiled at her, my throat constricting uncomfortably as my own eyes began to water.

She blinked the tears away.

"Oh, thank you. Where *have* you been?"

"I'm sorry, Naina. I'm so sorry." That was all I could manage lamely.

She said nothing. There was something strange about the way she looked at me and the way she lowered her eyes. Though she said nothing, her silence was filled with the words she longed to speak to me.

Unable to contain herself any longer, she put her arms around me, hugged me and whispered in my ear, "Where have you been? There was no news of you. I know you don't care for anyone, but you do know that someone cares for you. You must respect that, shouldn't you?"

I couldn't hold myself back. My arms went around her slender body. These feelings that were churning inside me were actually beautiful. I wanted to savour all of them, every one of them.

I took in the warmth of her hug, and it made me feel complete. My hands went around her, slowly.

"I got late trying to find the perfect gift for you," I whispered.

That was so dumb. But what else could I say?

I realized a moment later they were staring at us, the guests, watching us like mad hawks let loose.

"Naina, everyone is staring at us."

She let go, embarrassment sweating its way through the fingers with which she held me. Her moist eyes were still looking at me, waiting for an answer.

"I had gone to find myself, a part of me that I had never known existed within me," I said in a deep tone, and then smiled at her.

She stood puzzled, frowning, trying hard to understand the meaning underlying my words. I knew she was surprised because I had never talked such things before. We stood there in silence till her friends came running down the hall screaming, "Naina! Your cake, cake!"

I smiled, just as she did too.

She turned back to the room, to the table where a big chocolate cake was kept. Candles were sparkling on the cake, and their flames dancing gracefully, their worth fulfilled only when Naina, with her red, luscious lips blew them out one by one. This was followed by loud applause and the chanting of "Happy birthday, Nandy. Happy birthday. Happy birthday."

Her friends called her Nandy, and I disliked that. I liked to call her Naina. Only Naina.

I stood at the back, behind her friends, and sang the birthday song softly. Thoughts were crashing inside me, like wild maelstroms.

Naina cut a piece of cake and fed it to her mother. Everyone was laughing and talking, and the mood was of celebration. And then, the moment arrived. The guests were all giving their gifts. I inched away towards the back of the crowd. Soon, everyone was done.

Her eyes sought me out, and I walked toward her. I took the packet out of my pocket and gave it to her. She stared at it, the little packet. Tentatively, her fingers loosened the ribbons that bound it. She took out the tiny box inside and opened it. Speechlessly, she stared at what lay inside. Her eyes were wet. Her tears said it all. There were a million questions in her eyes when she brought them up to meet mine. And yet, there was also a glimmer of hope there.

There, nestled among the satin of the box was a diamond ring.

She looked at me with a feeling of consternation as it was beyond her imagination. She must have been hopeful of this to begin with, but with time, my actions must have killed her hope. She didn't say anything, but her eyes had a questioning look.

Before she could say something, I went down on my knees, took the ring from her, and said, "Naina, I love you."

She stared at me, speechless.

My own speech became more of a stutter as I tried to speak out the words that my heart wanted spoken.

"I love you, I love you Naina. Loving you has made me realize how beautiful life really is and how much I want to be a part of this world. The world which you are a part of."

I heard the other guests whispering, which grew louder and became a distinct noise. But I didn't avert my eyes from her lips, as I waited for her answer. She was taking a few moments. I heard Vikram saying from behind me, his voice hushed with surprise, "What happened to him?"

Even without looking, I knew they were staring at us for the second time that day, slack-jawed and open-mouthed.

"What's happening?"

"He's proposing."

"Omigod!"

"I told you, didn't I? They only pretend to be friends."

My eyes were still fixed on hers.

I was barely listening. She held my heart and life in her dainty hands.

And then, like a sun rising over the gloom, Naina smiled.

My heart soared.

Then she nodded, the smile flowing across her lips. I was overwhelmed, overcome with a euphoria I had never known or felt before. It was exaltation really, full of life, like a season of spring. I felt light, wrapped within the arm of love. The brittle loneliness that had been my armour for years, crumbled and fell around me. The face that had been bruised with solitude was now soothed by her smile. I looked at her; she was happy.

"I love you too," the words finally flowed out, marking her confirmation. She stretched her hand out, towards me.

I stoop up swiftly, took out the ring and put it onto her finger, embracing her right. I closed my eyes, and felt a sense of satisfaction, of completeness within me.

When I opened my eyes, I saw her parents smiling at us, pleased, but a little surprised. Their friends surrounded us, had come closer to us and were clapping and cheering us.

A few girls ran up to Naina and pulled her away from me, surrounded her, chattering like gleeful schoolgirls. The men came up to me, to congratulate me, to ask their questions about the sudden proposal.

"Guys, guys, listen! It's already a very big day for Naina. Let's make it bigger, shall we?" Nimmi announced.

The room rang with happy yells of "Yes!"

"Dance, dance, dance!"

I was jolted out of my euphoric stupor when Naina's mother suddenly took my hand. I couldn't read her expression as she did, but then, I'd never been able to do that. Her father was standing on one side, his expression as unreadable as his wife's. At least, she had managed a tentative smile.

"Dance," was all Naina's mother said to me.

I took Naina's hand and led her to the floor. We were lost there, while everyone danced around us, lost in each other. I can't remember if we said anything to one another. The music was slow, and I didn't know how to dance. I was embarrassed, but somehow held it back. I didn't want to lose the chance of being with her and dancing with her. Although we didn't hold each other too close, for it was too soon, we knew we wanted to in that moment; we would have wanted to hug each other and cry our hearts out.

It was 1 a.m. when people finally began to leave Naina's house. I was the last one.

2

A Secret Unravelled

It was quite late when I returned home. I headed to my bedroom, and then lay on the sofa. I was feeling blissful; like I had everything I ever needed. Now, I felt as in the lap of true love, wrapped within the care of my love Naina.

A few weeks later, it was just another day. I woke up at 11 a.m., not on my bed but on the leather sofa. I couldn't remember when I had fallen asleep. I jumped out of the sofa to stretch my aching body and then sat down again, sleepily.

I called for Kaka and asked him to bring in some orange juice. Then I went for a shower.

My juice was ready on the table, chilled to just the right temperature. I gulped it down in one go. My eyes fell on the photo album lying on my table. Old memories came rushing back to me.

This album had a photo of me with Naina, as she rested her head on my shoulder. It was clicked at an outing we had gone on with our friends. Everyone was clicking away, and Naina cornered me suddenly and stood close, asking Raj to take a picture of us. Raj asked us to smile, and I did so reluctantly. And then, just before he clicked, she placed her head on my shoulder. The photo had captured my surprise.

Later, Naina got the print developed and brought it to me. She had put it into this album.

I reached out and opened the album, and sure enough, there it was. The very first picture. Smiling, I lifted it to my face and kissed it.

There was a knock at the door just then; I remembered it was open. I almost dropped the album back on the table, embarrassed at the thought of someone seeing me kissing an album.

I turned to find Naina at the door. She had a knowing smile, a smile that told me that she had seen me kissing our picture.

Embarrassed and relieved at the same time, I said, "Oh, it's you. What are you doing at the door? Come right in."

She walked into my room and sat beside me on the sofa. I was still feeling a little uneasy, and so couldn't face her. I did smell her though – a clean and familiar a scent, one that gave me great pleasure. Her arm brushed against me, gently, and I felt something electric run within me. It wasn't the first time she had touched, but now, everything had changed between us.

"See, I was not even aware that I had slept on the couch last night. Now, my body is aching," I told her. "You're going to college now?"

"Duffer, our college is over," she smiled. But soon, with a rapid change in her facial expression and without saying anything else, she stopped. "Sorry," was all that came out.

"Sorry? Why?" I was a bit astonished.

"I called you duffer, that's why."

"Oh, come on! We love each other. That doesn't mean that we have to change for each other. We should love someone for who they really are. Why love someone who can't be themselves with you."

"Aw… that's so sweet." And she pulled at my cheeks, teasingly. I realized that I had spoken a little too much and a little too seriously about love.

"Oh, it's eleven. I have to get ready, or we will be late for college," I said, and I got up to move towards the bathroom.

"Duffer, today is a Sunday," she laughed. The sound of her merry laughter was light and unconcerned, and I understood that she had understood me.

"Oh, that's great. Then, there's no hurry. I can spend time with you here." And I sat down again, next to her.

"But our friends are waiting for us. Riddhima messaged me a while ago, said that we are meeting them, so we can hang out," she said.

"Whose treat?"

"Dutch."

"Okay, sounds great. And what time are they coming?"

"In an hour, I guess."

"Which means I get to spend one whole hour with you."

And this time when I smiled, there was no hesitation in my eyes. It was still peeping out through her eyes, though.

"Akshat, can I ask you one thing?" she asked, and I knew what was going on inside her.

"Hmm."

"How come you suddenly declared your love for me like that? I mean… last week when I came to see you, you had just disappeared without even a note or a message. And you have never been so vocal about liking me… you used to be so embarrassed when I held your hand. And now, suddenly, out of the blue, you say you love me. And that too in front of my parents and a whole lot of other people. What made you do that?"

I just smiled at her, "These things happen, Naina. I just realized I loved you and I wanted you to know that."

She pondered over that for a moment. But the floodgates to her heart had already opened.

"You know, when I came to your house last week and saw your door closed, I asked Kaka about you. He was genuinely surprised. He hadn't seen you that day. I thought you had left for college. But I couldn't find you there either. So I asked Vikram if he had seen you. Even he hadn't. I was so worried, you know. I asked everyone. No one had seen you. I was beside myself with worry. Where could I look for you? Later, Vikram asked me again if I had seen you. When I said no, he was worried too. He asked if I had checked with Kaka. I said I had, but that no one knew where you were. It was a nightmare…"

She stopped for a while, to catch her breath, and then continued, "I came to your house every day. I called you every hour… just to get some news about you. But nothing. And then one day, Kaka told me that you had informed your dad that you were out of the city and that you would be back soon. I felt like celebrating that day!"

I opened my mouth to say something to her, but no words came out.

"Finally, you came back. You are my life's most beautiful gift," her eyes filled with tears. My heart nearly broke. I could feel her pain.

I held her face, and looked into her eyes. She tried to smile but it came out weakly, faintly. She looked into my eyes. We could have sat like that for hours. I kissed her forehead and held her close, trying to take in all her pain, trying to take away the loneliness that she had felt those seven days.

"I'm back now, sweetheart. I'm back. I had to go away to realize how much you meant to me. Do you understand that?" I whispered.

She nodded against my chest.

"Everything is fine. I am back to live with you, to spend all my time with you. I love you very much. Sometimes one has to go far to come close. But I am back now, and I know what you mean to me. Isn't that great?" I whispered.

She nodded. We hugged each other for a long time, without saying anything, feeling the love and tenderness between us. When she let go, her tears had dried out. I tried to smile. She also made an attempt.

Naina got up and sat down in my lap. She put her hands around my neck and looked into my eyes. As I looked back at her, I could feel my face become warm with desire, could feel it glow, and I said, "Give me a kiss." She pressed her lips lightly to my left cheek.

"No, on my lips."

She came closer, and our lips were merely at a distance of a fingertip now. Her perfume filled my nostrils, made me feel heady. My arms went around her waist and hugged her tightly, as she put her lips over mine. She drew in my lips and we kissed. When she pulled herself away, I ran my fingers over her lips, then over her cheeks. When she was close to me, beside me, my face bloomed like a rose. And why shouldn't it be so? After years of loneliness, happiness and love were finally mine. She held me in her embrace and I wanted to be there for an entire lifetime.

"So tell me Akshat, where had you been all those days?"

"I will tell you some day," I told her. "See, it's getting late. Let me freshen up. Give me ten minutes," I kissed her again on her forehead and rushed for a bath.

"Alright. Mind if I look around?" she asked.

"It's all yours now sweetheart," I said, and moved towards the bathroom.

She stood up to take a stroll across the room. After looking at my album and remembering our moments together, she moved towards the window. She spent a few moments there, watching the empty road down below, and then went to my table. Many books and stationery stuff lay scattered on the table top, making it look messy. Realizing that the desk was in a state of disarray, she began arranging things automatically.

Her eyes went to the dairy, the red diary kept on the centre of the table, buried under books. She was surprised at the fact that Akshat kept a diary. So out of sheer curiosity, she picked it up. It never occurred to her that this was someone else's diary. To her, it was the diary of her beloved. Engrossed in the not-so-good handwriting, when she turned the next page, her eyes grew wide with shock.

I never intended to write this diary, but perhaps I am left with no choice. Loneliness has started consuming me. I want to say something, something about myself, but to whom? I had no idea whom to go to; nothing and no one else could be better than this diary.

Surprised by the sudden sadness the words evoked in her, she realized that she wanted to read more. She didn't want to tell Akshat about it, though, otherwise he would feel embarrassed and might not let her. She decided to take the diary and then replace it once she had read through.

She wanted to read it all now. But she knew she couldn't. There wasn't much time. She feared that I would come in any moment and would see her reading my diary. She whispered to the room, "Sorry, Akshat! I am taking you diary without asking you. I always wanted to know you. I don't know why I always saw an emptiness and loneliness in you, why you always try so hard to laugh and smile. This is the only way to know you. This will answer my questions about where you have been. And what made you realize love?" She slipped the dairy down into her shoulder bag quietly.

Just at that moment, I entered the room, fresh and energetic, dressed in a T-Shirt and faded jeans, and asked, "What happened to you?"

"Nothing, I was just wondering if we'll be able to reach on time. It's almost time," she said, slightly fidgety. This was the first time she had lied to me.

I knew she was fond of spending time with friends and was really looking forward to it. Although I was curious about her sudden strange expression, I didn't say anything about it.

"So shall we go?" I asked.

"Yeah," she said scanning me from top to bottom, and quickly added a "Looking good".

Only when I reached Corner House with Naina did I realize that our friends wanted the whole story from us. And that was the reason for the sudden get-together. They cast meaningful glances at us holding hands. And then there was a fusillade of questions, which I had a tough time dodging.

"Akshat, what happened to you?" Riya sniggered.

"What? What happened to me? Everything is fine," I said in a casual voice.

"You know what I mean. You proposed to Naina? We all were so shocked! Well, you guys getting together is great. Isn't it Arohan?" Riya said, nudging her boyfriend.

He nodded, chewing a piece of chilli-chicken he had been hanging on to for long, but didn't say anything.

"Alright, alright, explanation time. Akshat, spill the beans," said Vikram. I couldn't ignore that one, so I explained.

"Yes, I understand what you all want to know. But I could say that I missed her when I was away. Yeah, it's true that I should have proposed to her quite earlier but sometimes you know, it happens that everything that you look for is in front of you, but you don't understand it. It takes time. And so it was with me. You have to go away from someone in order to come closer to them," I said.

"Uh oh." Amidst groans and disappointment, the gang eventually accepted what I had said.

Nimmi, who was the funny one of the gang, poked Vikram and said, "Learn something from Akshat. Stop thinking about food for a change, and think about me." She made a face and everyone burst out laughing.

Every time I answered their questions, Naina stared at me, perhaps trying to decipher what I was saying, hoping that I would say something that would make her understand what might have happened with me in last seven days. But I disappointed her again, and answered the questions in an evasive way.

At the end of it, I realized that I too was enjoying this, for this was something that I had never done before. Everything had changed now. I have a life, I thought, and I smiled.

Naina wondered out loud, on seeing me smile, "What happened?"

"Nothing," I said and held her hand, which she responded to. "Just thinking, how big a duffer I was."

She laughed. When the party was over, I dropped Naina to her home; with our exchange of I love yous.

I remained there till she had gone inside the house, and then drove back to mine. I didn't think much about how quickly she had left: usually, we talked for a few moments before she took leave. Maybe she was tired; I didn't mind that too much.

As Naina entered the house, she was greeted by her mother. "Beta, how was your party? Did Akshat tell you anything?"

"Party was good, Mom. No, Akshat didn't say anything," she said, hurriedly, for she could no longer wait to start reading the diary which could answer all the questions that she had within her. "Mom, I am going to be in my room for a while. Please don't disturb me."

On entering her room, she locked it, threw aside her shoulder bag and pulled the diary out of it.

She fell on the bed, set her head against the pillow and opened the diary.

Naina took a deep breath and began reading.

3

A Captive Past

29th July, 2010

I never intended to write this diary, but perhaps I am left with no choice. Loneliness has started consuming me. I want to say something, something about myself, but to whom? I had no idea whom to go to; nothing and no one else could be better than this diary.

It was my 21st birthday. It was like every other year. I had a few friends around me. Mom and Dad came in for a while, though half-heartedly, as they were occupied with phone calls most of the time and then they left without much ado, leaving me in the company of my friends who too departed after cracking a couple of dirty jokes. It was around 12:30 pm when I bid goodbye to them. I still remember it was Naina who left the room in the very end, I didn't know why. Before leaving the room, she stayed at the door for more than a minute, casting her glance over me, smiling as she said, "Akshat, Happy birthday once again. Do let me know how you find my gift?" I just nodded and turned back to my room which was now filled with the gifts that had been given to me.

It was around 1 a.m. and Lucknow was letting off its steam in full blast as usual. Though my air conditioned room was pretty cold, I couldn't stop longing for fresh air. So I pulled up my chair to the balcony and found myself admiring the beauty of the silver moonlight that shone over the soft brown earth. After an hour of simply looking at the empty surroundings, I turned back to adjust my chair and sat down with a fresh novel to read. The light was yellow and dim, so dim that I could barely read it. After a few futile attempts, I gave up and kept the novel on the table by my side; but something was holding me from going inside. So, I simply stayed outside, taking in some more fresh air. It always soothed me, fresh air, took away all the tension I held inside. And I felt better. I turned on some music on my iPod and closed my eyes. But soon restlessness gripped me, again. I came back into my room. Since I couldn't think of anything else that could take me away from that feeling of emptiness, I decided to open the gifts. I was only interested in one.

I stared at it for a moment. It was an oblong package, neatly wrapped, with a card that said "Happy Birthday" in a delicate cursive writing. I tried to guess what lay inside, even weighed it in my hands many times to get an idea, but couldn't come up with anything. Tired, I loosened the ribbon and undid the decorated cover.

There was a box inside it. I opened it and found within it an album with the photos she had taken of us, each carefully labelled with captions. I realised it pretty late but I had been smiling all along. I turned its pages; saw every photo before keeping it aside. I was reminded again of those moments that had faded with time, and a deep nostalgia swept over me.

I still felt empty inside. I didn't even bother to open the other gifts.

It was definitely time to sleep, but an emptiness that stayed in my life stung me, kept me away from sleep. *Why? How many more sleepiness nights?* I asked myself. And that too, after one and half years. I was clueless. My mind and heart were pulled by the tentacles of my past, that had been buried somewhere deep inside within me. But memories and feelings, like drops of rain on windowsill, that run down even after the rains have stopped, remain with you, no matter how hard you have tried to bury it, to keep it out of your mind, heart or life, but it always clawed its way out. I decided to pen down my feelings on paper. It was, indeed, an instinctive and possibly right decision, because somewhere in my mind, although I didn't remember it, I had the idea to write about me.

I came to the table, adjusted it, and twisted the head of the table lamp so its light would fall on the paper that I pulled out from the piles that lay beside me. I sank into deep thought, started recalling and remembering the life that I had lived so far, and the paper swayed before me, for my restlessness kept forcing me to face this situation, to wrench away the tentacles of the past, and this struggle had started to tire me. But I decided that I had to put down my feelings somewhere: Easy to say, and to think, but difficult to write them. I thought a lot, but my mind couldn't decide on anything. Two hours had passed, and there wasn't a single line on that paper. I felt desperate. Thoughts bombarded me, but I never found a particular one to begin with.

My tenacity made me keep trying, and four hours had passed. However, luckily, words started to flow then from my pen.

When the inspiration to write was born in my mind, what could be a better subject to write about than myself?

Looking down at the paper, I fell into a silence, which became so long that it seemed I had begun to meditate. To falsify it, on the other hand, my mind was threading together another profound characterization of my own story which had begun earlier – but I never paid much attention to it.

To be honest, I couldn't recall my childhood. One thing that I remembered with utmost surety was that apart from money, I had possessed nothing. As far as I could recall it and as I had heard the story from the other servants in my house, there had been a lady, an old one, who had pampered me and had cared for me before fate intervened. I called her daima and she had died when I had turned eight. This had happened suddenly and had robbed me of everything I had. She had suffered from multiple organ failure. An oasis in the desert had dried. I could recall the last time that I had a good time with my family; it had been a month before her death.

I had been in Paris at that time, I had never wanted to go there, but since my nanny had been on leave at that time, I had been left with no choice. When I returned home, I had heard the news of her demise. It saddened me. I felt numb. I still am numb. It is like there is nothing in my life that I want to hold on to. Maybe, death is better. Oblivion to oblivion. And nothingness in between. Is that what my life is like? Why?

I still remember how much I missed her, missed her words of caution, of innocence and care. I didn't remember everything but I learnt through others, about her, came to know how passionately she had loved me. She had had no children of her own, and she had therefore treated me like her own. She always sat me on her lap, hugged me, and taught me good lessons to live life by. It was fun to remember some of the things that she would do for me, how she would pull me to the corner of my room whenever I wandered about, would wrap her arms around when I was scared or sleepy, run her fingers through my hair, and hold me to her chest to comfort me.

Whenever these memories would come to me, I would wince and shut my eyes as tightly as I could, but even after many attempts, I could not stop the tears that would roll down. I had with me a few photographs that I had taken with her. But that was not enough. Whenever my other servants spoke about her, it made me realize that my childhood had been made beautiful by her. From the moment I started to make sense of the world, had begun to understand it better, the world had felt terrible without her. An emptiness and loneliness had kept growing within me, no matter how much wealth I had, or my parents had. To avoid feeling this way, I tried to be with my own mother. She had always been busy though, with her kitty parties and with high society friends, and had hardly any time for me. It's true that people have time for unknown but not for family, not for the known. With the passage of time, my memories of childhood started to become fuzzy, and amid the altercations and disagreement between my parents. I started living alone, most of the time confined to my bedroom. On some days, I thought I was happy and being taken care of, but on others, I felt alone. I understood at a very early age that everyone wants to be loved and cared for all the time, and not just sometimes.

Life moved on and I grew up, but not everything in my life happened in the way I had hoped it would.

Things were normal with me, with what I felt, with how my hormones worked. By the time I was eighteen, my friends had started spending most of their time on their phones, talking softly, whispering even, not loud enough to be heard by anyone sitting beside them. But me? I was wandering towards some unknown variable, the pursuit of which was useful to me: academics and knowledge. It had been two years since she had left me. In those two years, I tried hard to fill the void that her absence had left behind. Who knew that I would be pursued to be loved by someone, and in return fall in love with her, an experience that would result in something life-changing, something that would open my eyes to life, that would change how I felt and thought, would change me into something that wouldn't be accepted by "normal" people, people around me, that even my parents would find me difficult to understand and live with, and that I would remain alone in this world, only immersed in doing something, anything, to fill the void in my life, to soothe the excruciating pain.

It was the tenth time that Ishita had hung up on my call. I was infuriated. My patience had started to fray, but I couldn't control the urge to call her again, and again. But one thing was for sure, even if she would answer the call, I would not be able to scream at her for she would either hang up again or talk rudely. When I called again, to my surprise, this time, the phone was unreachable. I understood. She had removed the SIM card from the phone. Clever of her, I thought. My nerves were razed with anger, but I knew I could do nothing but wait for her call. She might call in the evening, I thought. But based on her recent behaviour, my heart beat with palpitations of suspicion. It had started to smell foul, her actions, her love for me. And now, it was becoming too much for me to handle. I had to find out for myself what was going on with her. Twice earlier, I had thought about doing this but had dropped the plan. I suspected she was seeing someone else, but I wasn't sure about it. So, I had never brought it up with her. After a storm of thoughts in my head, at the end, I decided that I had to know the truth about her. I thought I would call her best friend and just ask. I searched her number on my phone, but realized that I didn't have it.

My suspicions were confirmed, were made real, when one day at the mall, I saw Ishita hanging out with someone else, another man. On asking around, I found out that she was with her boyfriend, and that Ishita was with me only for my money. When I confronted Ishita about this, she refused to answer my question. She kept giving excuses, and tried to prove herself innocent. She said she would give me the answers to all my questions on the following Wednesday. Many Wednesdays passed after that, but I got no answers from her. I called her up the first Wednesday, but all she gave me was an excuse again. She said, "I have an exam tomorrow. I can't speak to you now. I swear that I will tell you next Wednesday." And she had disconnected the phone, but not before I heard the sound of laughter behind her, the sound of a group of people laughing at me, mocking me. Things only got worse after that, and our conversations started becoming shorter, abusive. When I suggested that we don't call each other or speak to each other anymore, she accused me of cheating on her, of being with someone else. All I could do was hanging up on her, after I had cursed at her for accusing me of such heinous things. I had also threatened her, had told her that I would break up with her, but she didn't seem to care. Fed up with everything, I took a decision. I would break all contact with her.

Her betrayal had left me shattered, alone. I wished that someone would walk up to me and wipe away my tears, would hold my hands and say, "Life is beautiful. Live it." But no one came. I was all alone, surrounded only by a thick layer of silence- a silence that was going to eat away at me.

Days passed, and it seemed that seconds were crawling slower than a snail. Her memories made a heavy part of my brain, of my heart, and they were never wiped out completely. Expecting some calm, some compassion and support, but having no one to talk to, I soon acquired the habit of talking to myself. I listened to this voice that had started speaking from inside me and started spending a lots of time alone, in a corner of the room, trying to find the answers to all those unanswered questions, which never seemed to leave my mind.

Days slipped into weeks, and weeks into months. My life seemed stagnant. Some passing seconds took me away into the past, into blissful memories, but others took me to her betrayal, her amoral deed, made me to think in other ways about her, made me hate her, to forget her, to never forgive her. I knew that she spent her time with him. On the contrary, my life fell into silence and the trauma of this break up, I knew that I had to bear it on my own, although I needed someone to fill me with happiness.

Whenever my mind swam on lower tides, the void got filed with her malicious words and deeds. But every time I tried to shield myself against this, I found it very tough. Very tough for a person who was all alone, someone like me. I was reminded of how alone I had become. With constant revival of my life, my thoughts, my ideas led me to think that I was behaving well, but it never reflected in the way it should. The relationship had broken me, and I started disliking things that seemed like nonsense to me. I observed that I was surrounded by people with low morality. Whenever I tried to talk to them, I found myself more and more alienated from them. My so-called friends. And soon, to my surprise, I heard that people had started saying things about me – sometimes hurtful, sometimes boring, sometimes philosophical, and sometimes obnoxious. I never paid much attention to them and accepted their gossip gracefully. One thing was for sure, if you talked like them, behaved in their ways, they thought you were a great friend. I disliked such company and started spending much time with myself, without any care or opinion towards others' problems and lives. In a world of people who considered me eccentric, I was left with a very few friends to talk to.

It's been truly said that if you don't pay any heed to your friends' words when you are despairing, it will be difficult for you to swim out of the loneliness. And when you don't try to help yourself, nobody else does. After a few persistent efforts, your friends begin to leave. That was what I began observing at the beginning of July. I was alone; I renounced everything, even my mobile phone. I realised that a major obstacle in my pursuit of everything was my wish to have someone close to me and with whom I could share everything. But this dark phase of my life was not yet ready to get over, and it left me alone for months like this, without anyone to call m own, Living like this, sometimes, made me question if I really did deserve a life like this? Was this all my fault? And such questions always generated insecurity in me, reduced my confidence and made me feel guilty.

Things never happened the way I wanted them to. Nevertheless, I kept myself reserved and didn't mingle with many friends. Because of only one reason – their nonsensical actions. I observed that none of the friends in the group, who often met in the evenings, ever discussed anything useful. They spoke only about porn, girls and other useless things that they considered enjoyment.

One night, two of my friends were working on some class project. But after writing some slides, they started their usual useless talks. But when I didn't participate in that, one of them remarked that I don't enjoy life and then added that keeping a long, serious face results in nothing, and that man can't achieve anything living like this. Though the remark was made without any intention to hurt and was said in humour, I took these lines to mean something else.

With each passing day, I began talking to myself all the more, regardless of whether it was college time, lunch time or dinner time. I started taking a stroll in the ground alone just after dinner and justifying everything. I had found a voice and the best way to convince myself was through self conversation. I was surprised over time, that I could have access to that voice, my own understanding voice every time. Even when her thoughts flashed back to make me to suffer, the calm, confident and compassionate voice was always with me.

With time, my day-to-day focus was trudging its way through the tangled web that was my life. It felt like a treadmill that got you nowhere. After constant analyzing, I came to the conclusion that I was not doing things that made me happy, that would bring joy to me. And my life was not moving in a direction that would help me find myself, help explore happiness after such setback, which was indeed a difficult task. I was determined to change my life and started putting all my effort to achieve whatever I wanted in my life. As I began, it seemed that each moment had become a celebration for me. There was a rush of energy and I immersed myself into it.

Now, I began noticing Naina's eyes on me when we were together; I always found myself liking her attention and friendly gestures. She was the only one to stand by me in all of this. She probably understood more than she let slip through her words and expressions. She was a good friend. Whenever she was with me, I felt good. A little hopeful. I thought and tried to recall the exact moment when we had met for the first time. It was the first day of the 3rd semester.

In this semester, separate sections for different branches were made. Everyone was rushing towards the notice board to check their name and the respective sections. I also checked my name. It was section A.

After checking my name, as usual, I entered the canteen. But that day, I guess, I was a little early. It was around noon and the sun was scorching. I was dripping with sweat and I took a glass of soda. After sometime little while, two of my friends came in. So we all decided what to eat and I went ahead to place the order.

While they sat chatting about inanities, I was trying to read notes. I was used to the light whispers wafting over the premises and it had become a habit for me now. It was only when some loud noise or laughter broke my concentration that I raised my eyes to seek out the cause.

It was the third time that I had raised my eyes in a disappointing way, but just when I was to going to turn my gaze back to the pages in my hand, my eyes spotted her. She was just entering the crowded café. I took a quick glance at her as she smoothly passed between and around groups of people. My eyes settled on her fine, slim and shapely figure. She had a delicate, chiselled face with graceful black eyebrows, angled like the wings of a seagull, in perfect contrast to her fair and smooth complexion and sharp nose. Her black, shiny and silky hair gave her a look of elegance, falling down her back, a small wisp of hair resting on her forehead, which she sometimes pushed to the space behind the ears. Her ear rings were long, dangling and shining brightly against the lights of the café, which added an incredible charm to her beauty.

I decided to avert my eyes, to go back to reading the pages, but before I could do this, I took another covert glance at her; I was intrigued by the way she held herself. I noticed she was alone, she hadn't spoken to anyone so far and was wearing a peacock blue salwar kameez. This made her stand out all the more because every other girl was clad in either jeans or skirts.

As I watched her, I gauged my own appearance. I was of normal height, a twenty-two-year-old. My physique was well-taken care of, my biceps had thickened over the years. I looked nothing like I used to in the first year of college, thin and frail, with rimless spectacles hanging on my nose. Now, I was properly shaved, and my hair was perfectly styled. My Van Heusen shirt and trousers, branded shoes, and a Rado watch on my wrist suggested my prosperity and metropolitan affluence.

I got back to my pages and took sips of my coffee. After a few seconds I looked up from behind my coffee cup and saw her coming towards my side. She held a tray with a cup of coffee on it, and was trying to manoeuvre the cup through the crowded people. She kept uttering, "Excuse me, excuse me" ever so softly to make her way through the crowd. But a boy beside her moved his hand abruptly, almost hitting her arm. She turned her wrist quickly enough to make sure that most of the coffee spilled onto the tray, but her high-heeled sandals betrayed her and she couldn't prevent a big drop landing on my papers.

"Oh, I am so sorry!" she was mortified and kept the tray down quickly. Immediately conjuring a handful of tissues, she started wiping the coffee blot off, "Let me help you to clean up."

I didn't say anything and tossed the ruined paper into a nearby dustbin. I looked at her, her face which was still showing that she was sorry. I tried to relax it and said, "Oh! Don't worry and don't feel sorry. It happens, especially in a crowded canteen and among idiots who never look around."

"Okay, hope you don't mind it."

"No, its fine," I said. After looking at her from head to toe, I asked her, "So, computer science student?"

She smiled, or better put, tried to smile. A fake smile of assurance passed over her face, and she tried to look nonchalant, but then, she opened her eyes with little amazement and asked, "How do you know?"

"About what?"

"Umm.. That I belong to computer science. You look very observant. Or is it because you might know me? Or was it just an intelligent guess?"

I smiled before I said, "Oh, first a guess, then by observation. A little part of your book is peeping out of your bag. Red. I have the same book. But now, looking at your expression, I think I am right." I showed her my book.

"Yeah, you are absolutely right," she smiled. "Umm, can I sit here, if you don't mind, Akshat?"

"Oh, sure! Please make yourself comfortable," I said. And then it struck me. "One minute, you just called me by my name. How do you know me? I have seen you for the first time."

"Oh," she mumbled and was about to sit, but my abrupt question stopped her from doing so. "Lots of people know about you. You were the topper in the last two semesters. I saw you for the first time when you received the prize last college day."

"Okay," I was surprised that people had noticed me, and I was lost for a moment. It was sheer bad luck that the two people who should have noticed me the most, paid any attention towards me, or known that I was performing well in the college were just not bothered. Giving money and assurances of time was all they could manage.

I heard a click of her fingers. "Excuse me. Can I sit here? I don't see an empty seat anywhere else."

"Sorry, yes please," I managed, coming out of my daze. "And sorry, but I won't pay for you."

"Sorry? I don't get you," she looked so lost.

"Your coffee," I said sipping my tea and indicated towards her tray.

"Oh! Don't worry," and we broke into laughter together.

She sat opposite to me and dragged her tray. "Wow! You are quite observant," she said, with a feigning admiration. "You are a very interesting person. Let's begin this from the beginning. Hi, I am Naina Bhagat Malhotra." She put forth her hand towards me.

I shook hands and responded in little lower tone, "Hi. I am Akshat Diwan."

After so many months, I too was feeling good about this conversation. I made no efforts to keep it brief; rather, I tried to prolong it.

"Then let me amaze you a bit more. You are a dancer too, right?" I said, with an intention to cause her more surprise.

And I was correct when I saw a frown of puzzlement on her forehead. She asked with wide, shocked eyes, "How do you know about this? I don't think I am carrying anything that could have made you guess *that*. Or did you see me perform on stage?"

I was constantly smiling and said, "Umm...yes. What a great performance!"

"Really?"

"No, sorry. It's just that when your high heeled stilettos betrayed you, the way you controlled yourself in just a moment... only a dancer can do that. Am I right?"

Her mouth formed an "O" and her eyes went wide. "Now, how could you know that? Did you see me perform on College Day by any chance?... Absolutely. Hundred percent. I think this evening is quite wonderful. You know everything about me without having me say anything."

"No, I didn't see you performing. I was watching the way you walk so easily in those stilettos. There is a controlled grace about the way you move… got me thinking that you had to be a dancer."

She blushed ever so slightly and I smiled at her, earnestly and with obvious enthusiasm. And her brooding eyes pierced into mine and asked very sweetly, "We are going to become great friends."

"Yeah, we can be! But it depends," I said. A lovely radiant joy filled my face.

"Depends on?" she gave me a quizzical look.

"Nothing, let's leave that for now," I said, taking the last sip of coffee. But her look surely was suffused with a sense of satisfaction. The good part was, despite her curiosity, she didn't ask anything after that.

This was our casual meeting.

Yes, she was in my class in 3rd semester. With time, our meeting turned into friendship. And I found her a really good friend, different from most others I knew. Sensible, smart and always positive. Our mutual friendship, it seemed, started turning into something more than friendship. We talked most of the time, but there were never any declarations of love. From anyone's side.

At first, I had nothing in my mind and didn't have any wish that we should talk further, but in class, we exchanged a few casual hellos. Over time, I noticed that our talks grew longer, and she spoke and responded to each and every word with great care, always keeping a smile on her face.

It started making me comfortable, and, to my surprise, in spite of having so many friends in our group, she usually spent most of her time with me. I found solace in her. I never hesitated to call her, whether it was early morning or class time. I smiled over this observation about her. She was the kind of friend who made my life a whole lot easier and understood me very easily. I also understood her. There were times that I didn't care for her words, but surprisingly, she never thought badly of me.

The depression and loneliness did rush into my life on some days, making me miserable. I didn't know what to do. I just sat alone for hours, didn't know where I was looking, but kept staring into open spaces. I didn't want to live like this. I wanted to regain the joy in my life, but didn't know how or when it would come. I was trying very hard to collect the broken pieces of life, trying to put them together. But it always left a void inside me.

It seemed someone held the key to my happiness, and it wasn't me. Many pages of fate were to be added in between the two of us – me and Naina – before I shall understand her, before we shall be together. Perhaps I was not ready for any rollercoaster ride yet, but like I had said, someone else was moving and adjusting the gears of my life.

Then one day, I did something that I never wanted to do. I was left with no option but to do just that.

4

Nocturnal Journeys

Seven days earlier

It was unusually quiet when I returned home that evening. It was the last day of college. I asked Kaka where my parents were. He said despondently, "They've not come back since morning."

I had anticipated as much.

I went into my room and locked the door from within. I sat at my window staring at the falling dusk.

They had had another fight this morning. It was just more serious this time. In fact, it was more serious than any of their previous fights. They had actually raised their voices. There had been the sound of glass crashing. My dad had flung a porcelain vase at the wall in anger. The word "divorce" hung in the air. That one word coloured my whole day. As luck would have it, I didn't meet Naina that day in college. All for the better. I didn't want to infect her gaiety with my despondence.

They had banged doors and rushed out of the house in their respective cars. That day, the walls I had built around myself had come crashing down around me. I knew that this life was a farce. My parents might be divorced soon. Where would I stay then?

Of course, I am 21, so I can choose to live where I want. But how could I choose between two strangers?

I realized that I would have to leave this house. I needed answers and I couldn't find them here or anywhere. I needed to get away from this claustrophobic mess so that I could focus on my life and understand where I wanted to head.

"Why do they not try to understand each other? At least for me?" I asked myself but I knew that it was useless thinking over this. Sometimes it really chagrined me; sometimes it filled me with rage. "Why don't they divorce rather than killing each other every other day? It will be a relief for all."

Soon, I started feeling that I couldn't live in this situation from now on and made my mind to leave home for a few days. When this idea crawled into my mind, it filled me with relief. Without thinking about anything else, I started packing my bag: two sets of clothes, a towel, credit cards, ATM cards and a few warm clothes. I left the mobile on the table. When I walked out, a few servants looked at me, saluted me in deference and smiled at me. I too reciprocated, without showing any expression of stealth or anger on my face. As usual, they didn't ask anything.

It was evening but darkness had already filled the sky. Few stars sparkled and the moon was glowing. I had mostly travelled by air all my life. Thankfully, those one or two occasions when I did board the train helped me remember the way to the station. I flagged down a taxi and reached the station. I overpaid him as usual, and then I remembered that I would have to stop doing that soon.

After reaching there, I looked all around, taken aback on seeing the crowd. I was coming to the railway station after many years and its memories had faded now. I didn't know what to do, where to go. So, I just sat at the nearby bench and kept looking at others. It wouldn't have been more than ten minutes when a train whistled, signalling its start. It was on the same platform where I was sitting. I looked towards that train and in next moments, it started dragging itself away from the station slowly. People were rushing towards the train, in the fear of getting left behind. As I had no other plan and it was getting cold, without another thought, I boarded the train without knowing where it was going. *Who cares!* I just wanted to go away from this place, away from the arguments, the shouting, and the noise.

I hadn't even realized that I was required to book a ticket for the air-conditioned compartment well in advance. I never booked tickets anyway; it was all done by my dad's employees. I had no way of remembering such details.

I hopped onto the train and landed in a sleeper compartment. I kept walking, looking for an empty seat. Luckily, I reached a compartment occupied by a very few passengers. I threw the bag on the opposite seat and sat beside the window.

Once seated, I looked outside, silently watching the station pass. Rushing and shouting people, coolies carrying the luggage, and several vendors selling their stuff comprised the hubbub on the platform.

As the platform faded away from sight, and the station was left behind, the train picked up more speed. I adjusted myself into the seat, and put my head against the railings of the window. I could barely see anything outside for it was dark, but I could fathom the silhouettes of trees and shrubs. The monotonous sounds of the moving wheels on the tracks gave me comfort. I didn't know where this train was heading but without making any effort to know this, I remained there and stretched my legs.

With the slight breeze ruffling my hair and caressing my cheeks, my eyelids started to droop with fatigue and I closed my eyes. Soon, my mind wandered to the events of this morning.

There were so many whys tormenting me.

Why do people get married when they don't want to live with each other?

Why do people who can't stand each other even get married? Maybe, my parents had been in love once… long ago, before I was born. Maybe not. I am not too sure. But I had never seen even one caring word exchanged between them for as long as I can remember. I remembered though that theirs was merely a marriage of convenience. Daima had said that once. And then, as if she had uttered blasphemy, she had sealed her lips shut, refusing to elaborate. I had eased the story out of her in bits and parts over the course of a month.

My father was the last heir to inherit the vast fortune of his ancestors in Rajasthan. He was born into money. My mother was from an equally illustrious lineage. My dad had fallen in love with a girl from a poor family, and poor only in comparison. That girl was well educated and walked with the times; she reciprocated his feelings. My father spoke to my grandfather about this and said he wanted to marry this girl. But my grandfather, who had been keeping tabs on my father, said he would hear of no such thing. If my father wanted to marry this girl, he would be cut off from the family money. He would have to fend for himself. My father was young then. And brash. He left the house. But when he went to meet the girl, he was told that she was being married off to a man her parents had chosen for her.

My father went straight to the marriage *mandap* and found that the wedding was already over. The girl was crying, but when she saw my father, the despair in her eyes came out in her tears.

He had no answer to her questions. He looked at the groom closely. It was my grandfathers' office peon. Shaken beyond belief and numb with outrage, he decided never to talk to his parents again. He knew well that the girl would have been married to a better educated man if it wasn't the influence of his own father and the pressure he must have put on the poor family.

He went off to Lucknow to his friend with whom he shared a good relationship. He made all his wealth single-handedly and from scratch. He became a well-known business tycoon within five years. Repeated letters about my grandfather's failing health did not persuade him to return to Rajasthan. But one letter, which said that his mother was no more, made him come back.

He was surprised to see that my grandfather too was on his deathbed. My grandfather left him a will, leaving all his money to my father's son, which would be me. A year later, my father married a woman over a business deal. Within a year of their marriage, I was born.

My mother had been in love with someone else, but her father had wanted the business deal badly. So she hadn't been given a choice in the matter either.

When I was born, I was just baggage to them. Unwanted baggage.

And that is why Daima became the centre of my universe.

Even now, I craved for happiness. It seemed that happiness was beyond my reach and the things which I possessed – money, social status and endless parade of splendour – were not in a mood to give me my share of happiness. Though Naina's company still worked like balm on my wounds, I didn't have enough courage to go ahead and reciprocate in the same way.

That morning again, I had felt exasperated and had left the room, hearing the same argument between my parents, and had come to my room. The sun had come up in the sky, almost enough to lighten the world, and in it I found my own pleasure, as it always made me feel joyous. The summer sun is scorching, but the mild warmth of love is always soft. It was only scorching heat of a feigned relationship between my parents; it could have been pleasant if I had enjoyed the love of my parents. But sadly, they had no love for each other, and as a result, none for me too. I tried to enjoy the warm sunlight, in an effort of trying to make the best out of what was available, and pulled away the window curtain, welcoming the sun's rays to fall into my room properly.

The sun brought back the same feelings that I had been dodging for the past few years: why did my parents get married when they were not happy together? Such questions perplexed me, always left me answerless. Even though I was well aware of the fact that I would remain clueless, I still kept asking the same questions.

I was barely in my early twenties. I had a palatial home; high standard of living was what defined me from the outside. And it was only a dream for many others to live such a life. But it was only me who knew the hollowness beneath this richness. How sometimes life plays the smartest of tricks on you and guiles you. It endowed me with everything that any person would love to have, but left me unhappy nonetheless.

All my friends say I am a good guy, and a lucky one too. I could have agreed with the first appreciation, but definitely not with the second one. Yes, I didn't deny the fact that I had everything – fame, name, money and power – that too at a young age, but it was not the amazing and spectacular life that they fancied it would be. I believed that if I could have been given the poor but joyous life that they had, maybe then I could have been valued more and loved more. I had people running around me for my money, not for the person I was.

There were times I consoled myself with the thought that everything would become fine with time. But time, unfortunately, didn't make it easy; it only made things worse. Till three years ago, it had been easy to ignore all this. But it was impossible now. A sickness had started to roll within me, seeing my parents. *Why* do they always fight? *Why* don't they remember the most beautiful moments that they have lived together? But these questions were of no use. Whenever I dreamt that things will get better, and believed that the next day everything would be fine between them, that I would be something for them rather than another person living in such a palatial house, things remained the same. Each morning began with same cursing and taunting at each other, with me as witness at the dining table. Things never changed.

I have heard many say that couples get habituated with everything, if given enough time. Generally, such a statement is meant to motivate someone; but in my case, it meant the opposite.

Though my eyes were closed, the heavy thoughts added an unimaginable restlessness to it. I checked my Rolex watch for the time. Yes, I wore a Rolex. I had changed my Rado because the bright and catchy dial disturbed me. My life was not as bright and it made me uncomfortable. So this Rolex, subtle and expensive. I had enough money to waste on such useless things. I realized it was time to go to the dining table for breakfast. I knew the cook would have placed the food properly on the table, everything that I loved to eat. I stood up from the chair by the window, shuffled across the room and without any other thought on my mind, except one: my parents might have become nice to each other by now, and were waiting for me at the table.

Usually, for as long as I can remember, food was placed and arranged on plates on the empty dining table. The cooks smiled as I approached the table. I reciprocated with the same warmth and exchanged the greeting. But they, as well as myself, both knew the same old story- my parents would not be present. They all knew what I went through daily. Initially I used to ask them, and they would reply; but with passage of time, I stopped asking. My eyes held the questions, theirs the same answer.

As I came near and sat down, I heard muffled but shrill sounds of arguing from the room on the first floor, the room on the right where the staircase ends. I knew exactly who was making those sounds.

It was something different, something dangerous this time. I looked at the room curiously. A spirited argument was in progress, continuously growing with each passing second. I couldn't hear the exact words because of the closed door and their words remained muffled and indistinct, but at the last moment, I sensed the pulling of chairs, the banging of the door and a female voice rising in rage, uttering words I was only partly able to understand. I understand that it was abusive, loud and furious, but ending with a sob of pleading which surprised me. I didn't understand what was going on. It was then that some china dishes crashed and shattered against the wall.

I rushed towards the staircase, leaving my breakfast on the table, but it was of no use. A minute later, as I reached the room, the door flew open and out came my father, face ablaze with anger and his breath raspy and uneven. I remained frozen where I was.

My father left the house soon after; drove away in his BMW.

I was perplexed about the situation, felt a little baffled because it was not something that happened every day. It was something violent even for my parents.

At this age, I should have been dating girls and having the time of my life. But I was not doing anything of that sort. Why? Answers were very simple and clearly visible. Though I had lots of boys and girls accompanying me all the time, it wouldn't be fair to call them friends. Why should I, especially when all they were seeing in me was my financial status? Isn't it true that when something is no longer useful to you, it interest others?

My physical appearance communicated my status. My built and sturdy muscles, my clothes and accessories among other things clearly suggest my prosperity and affluence. My friends said that I was handsome, but I never did care about it. Almost everyone was dating and were involved in relationships, while I remained single. The reason of course was not because there was dearth of beautiful girls, but because I stayed away from all that. And that wasn't my fault for sure, I knew. Why would it be my fault when people, most often than not, chose me, not for me, but for my money? But sometimes, or I would say most of times, I felt lonely. And sometimes in the moments of silence and prelude, I wondered if I was destined to be alone forever, destined to not get the real affection of anyone.

There always came mixed feelings for me. On one side, I felt such things but on the other side, I also felt that it was best living a single, uncomplicated life. I asked myself, "Why have things become this way – at home as well as outside it?" When the feeling prolonged over time, it turned into resentment.

That's how I came to hate romance so deeply, and all else associated with it. Holding hands, sending love messages, buying small things, etc., did not really appeal to me. In short, I had started hating everything that was related to the word love, even remotely so. But sometimes, just about a few times, I had urged with myself in favour of those feelings. I also wanted to feel the warmth but was scared. So then, back to square one.

Vikram had asked if I had wanted to have dinner or to hang out somewhere, in a lounge or discotheque. I had declined that day. It was not that I always declined such things and decided to live in agony, but since that morning, my mood had been off. Even Avantika and Riddhima had asked, but I had turned them down as well. Judging me over several times, Naina hadn't said a word but had only cast her glance over me. All of them understood that something terrible had happened that morning, or maybe they just pretended to have understood.

I left when they all drove towards some disco, making their plans to enjoy the evening. Though I didn't consider myself a sharp observer, I noticed to my surprise that whenever I had decided to cut myself out of the fun, Naina had also left with me so that I could drop her. She always came up with such brilliant reasons that no one ever argued or countered with her.

The memories of Naina created a whole new set of tumultuous emotions within me. As I tried hard to consciously erase all thoughts, I could hear the sound of the train running on the rails again. Noisy. Fast. Echoing. I started enjoying the motion of the train. The wind hitting my face was now cold and harsh. So, I closed the window. But as soon as the sound died out, my mind went back to another conversation which had happened a few days ago.

"Hey Akshat, what do you think?" Nimmi asked.

"About what?"

"About love. I mean, you know that Naina loves you, right? I love Vikram. He loves me. Tell me what you think about love."

"What?" I am sure my face looked as baffled as I was feeling on the inside.

She smiled and said, "She will never tell you, I guess, but she loves you. Oww!" She broke off as Naina elbowed her in the ribs.

"Shut up!" she hissed.

"She's kidding," said Naina. She didn't look up at me.

Out of some perverse feeling, I said, "Love is just a time-pass word. There is nothing called true love. Lies! That is all love is… lies. And people just use this word as a joke."

I ignored the shocked gasps my response generated.

"What?" asked Nimmi.

"That's what I think about love."

"Oh, but… but… it's not like that at all. Love is a happy and awesome feeling," Nimmi said, trying to defend herself. "See, Vikram and I are in love and so happy together." She clutched Vikram's arm.

"For how long?" I asked.

"What do you mean how long? Love is forever!" she beamed, but now there was an edge to her voice.

"It's not. What do you guys do? You kiss, you fool around, you feel each other up, and you think that is love? And then what happens? Everyone knows. Either you will cheat on him or he will cheat on you. Then you will start hurting each other without remembering the beautiful days you had spent together. And later, you won't even like to see each other. That's love."

Enraged now, Nimmi blurted out, "Just because you got ditched, you think life is going to cheat all of us? You are such a coward!"

She stomped off with that and Vikram went after her, trying to calm her down.

I was a little shocked at her underhandedness. How could she use my break-up to win her pointless debate!

"Did I say something wrong?" I asked everyone, looking at nobody in particular, especially not Naina. No one said a word.

I looked at their frozen faces. They all began eating and talking, pretending that the scene had never happened. And then they all began to leave, one by one. No one bothered to say bye.

Naina was the only one left.

"Why did you say that? You hurt her."

"I didn't say anything wrong. Did I?"

"It's your perception. You can't generalize this."

"It's the reality I see all around me. One needs to accept it because one can't hide or run away from reality."

"Say sorry to Nimmi," she said.

"Ok, if you say so. I will say sorry."

"That's good. Let's go. They might be downstairs."

I nodded and we went downstairs.

Before we could go speak to Nimmi and Vikram, Naina asked, "Why don't you believe in love?"

I didn't say anything. She didn't pursue the matter. I apologized. We parted.

5

The Pilgrim

The train came to a halt. I must have dozed off, but the mad dash of people going out and getting into the train woke me up. It must have been a comparatively bigger station than all other s we had passed. The lights, stalls, rushing people, and coolies indicated that it was abuzz with activity. I instinctively tried to direct my eyes on the stone-marker where the place's name would be mentioned, but I couldn't see it properly because there was no light.

Yawning, I looked at my watch; four hours had passed. There was rustling of feet around me and the sound of bags being dragged. A few people had occupied the front berth just opposite mine, others were putting their luggage below the berth.

I yawned again, and pulled out my bag for a water bottle. As I was putting it back again, a heavy-built man startled me with his loud question, "Excuse me? This is my seat. S2-32."

I looked at him; blank. I tried to understand what he had just said. Before I could speak anything, he spoke again, "Can I see your ticket?"

He must have thought I'd produce a ticket, but without saying a single word, I stood up, made my way through the passengers still trying to find their seats and vendors trying to sell their stuff.

I heard his voice again, answering some woman who asked him about who the boy was.

"Some mad boy," he had said.

He was right, I was mad. Mad with the complexity of love, life and relationships and mad with the effort of trying to make sense out of it all. Without caring too much about his words, I stepped out on the platform.

I was still wondering which station it was, and then I stopped one vendor selling roasted *masala chana*. I was slightly hungry too, but ignored that bit for a moment and asked him, "Which station is this, *bhaiya*?" I asked politely.

First, he stared at me, his expression ensuring me he considered me lost. " Varanasi," he said quickly and moved on.

I spotted a wooden bench and headed towards it. Varanasi had always been synonymous for *pundits, artis,* temples and such things. Maybe a lot of crowd too. No wonder so many people were getting on to the train and off it too. I was starving, so bought a packet of chips and a cold drink. The whole platform was bathed in the milky light of a tube light. There weren't several people on the platform, probably because it was late at night. I didn't have an idea as to what I should do and where I should go. For a moment, I felt afraid, and almost muttered a curse at myself for running away from home.

Just then, a man came and sat next to me on the bench. He looked old, pretty old. His long salt and pepper beard, wrinkled hands, and slow pace of approaching the bench confirmed that. He must have heard the muttering; he was staring in my direction. I looked up into his eyes, sure that giving him a dirty look would take his eyes off me. But the penetrating gaze held me, and before I could gather, he smiled and said softly, "Your time is about to change, young man. The next few days will change everything you have known." I was perplexed to say the least.

My reverie was broken by the whistle of the train on the platform right behind me, signalling departure. The man was still smiling through his eyes and I was glued to him for some unfathomable reason. His eyes twinkled when he said, "Don't miss this one. It's time." The other train was going to go; he could have been talking about the train. He could have been talking about my life. I picked up my bag and got up, swiftly walking towards the other train. Why I didn't go to the one I had hopped out of, I cannot say.

I entered the air-conditioned coach this time. Then thinking about the mysterious man, I looked at the bench again. He was gone. Vanished. I walked into the almost empty compartment found an empty seat opposite a young chap reading a novel. I didn't pay much attention to him, threw my bag on the lower seat, and prepared to lie down. That's when I saw the book he was reading: *A New Beginning.* The back to back ominous events disturbed me.

The trained rumbled and bellowed loudly to signal that it had started. The train had barely been in motion for about ten minutes that it slowed down again. Finally, the train stopped with a pneumatic hiss, halted so quickly it stirred the bogies violently. Both of us had to hold ourselves against the seats and whatever we could lay our hands on. It was definitely not a station and the brake was sudden.

I looked at the man before me, but there were no reaction. The person tried to look outside through the window glass, and then muttered, "Someone pulled the chain. Must not be interested in letting the train reach Delhi in time." With that, he settled upon his seat, resuming his novel. I emulated him, telling myself this must be routine stuff. So, I lay down again and closed my eyes.

"Ticket please," hearing this, I opened my eyes. It was the ticket checker, dressed in his black coat. He looked at me and asked again, "Ticket please?"

I didn't have the ticket. That scared me for a while. I looked outside. It was quite dark and I was somewhere in between stations. *What if he asked me to get down here?* Realizing this, my face fell. From the corner of my eyes, I glanced over at the man who was sitting on the opposite berth. He was looking at me, but his face was calm.

"No ticket?" he asked again, writing something on the papers he was carrying.

"Umm...no. I don't have a ticket," I stammered. I had never experienced such a situation in my life before.

The TC frowned at me and then sat down beside me. "You have to pay a fine. You seem to be an educated student. Don't you know that travelling without ticket is an offence?"

I didn't reply. I was really not in any mood to talk. I just wanted to get out of the situation.

"From which station have you boarded the train?" He asked, keeping the paper aside and taking out a receipt book from his pocket.

"Umm, Varanasi," I said softly, only barely audible to him.

"And where will you get down?" he asked, briefly looking at me and then writing something on the paper.

I grew puzzled as I wasn't aware of where this train was heading. The man had said something about Delhi, so I took the chance.

"Delhi."

It was quite expected that the man opposite me would get interested in this situation. He said in an easy tone, "The train is almost empty, TC *sahab*. Please make a ticket for him."

"Yes, please," I added softly.

"Okay," said the TC, but his tone didn't seem very convinced. He wrote something on the paper, calculated the fare and tore out the ticket.

"Two thousand five hundred, with fine," he said.

I opened my bag, and pulled out the money. He handed over my ticket to me, examined the ticket of the other man and then left.

I arranged my bag and looked at him.

"Thanks for your help," I said with gratitude.

He smiled for the first time, "Don't mention it."

He was looking at me intently. "So, have you run away from home?" he asked.

"No, why would I?" I suppressed my tone.

"Did you thank me for convincing the TC or mentioning Delhi? You are sweating in an air-conditioned coach!" He said wisely.

I knew defending me any longer would be foolish and what would be the harm in sharing with someone who I won't ever meet again. "Yeah, I didn't know where this train was going, until you said it. I just boarded this train because it was the first one to leave the platform. And yes, I am running away from home."

"Look at your clothes, shoes, bag and watch! I can see you belong to a rich family. I hope it's not for a girl.'

"Why? Rich boys can't fall in love?"

"No, I didn't say that. I just made a comment on what

happens in society these days. The rich just flaunt their money to impress others; don't really care for anyone or anything. Not for emotions, not for feelings. Everything can be bought with their money."

"You could be right. But I don't belong to that category."

"Oh, then you girlfriend dumped you?"

"I didn't say that."

"Neither have you disagreed with it."

"No girl dumped me; I just found out that she was with me for my money. One day, I found her cheating on me, and then she was gone. I didn't make any attempt to get back with her after that. But it was terrible, you know. And your words are somehow quite appropriate. People do come to you because you have money to spend for them."

"Hmm. If you saw through it, then why did you leave your home? You seem to have come to terms with the break-up pretty well, I gather."

"Yes, I am just in pursuit of solace. I don't think there is something called love in this world."

"Why would you say so? Please excuse me, but if someone bad leaves you, has cheated you in the name of love, it doesn't make sense to say that love doesn't exist at all. Especially based on just one incident."

"You know my parents had been in love once. But after marriage, they fight like cats and dogs. Now what would you say?"

He remained silent for a few minutes, and then spoke after some deliberation.

"It's not *always* like that. But yes, sometimes, it happens with the best of us."

His calm tone made me lower my voice. "I cannot believe love is eternal. It seems like the love that was depicted in their old photographs has just vanished."

"I empathize. But I truly feel that for a successful marriage, one has to fall in love with his or her partner over and over again."

"Really? Do you feel that way for your wife?" I asked, still sarcastically.

"Yes, I love her so much," he said, and a smile crawled to his lips. Soon, his face was suffused with the memory and warm moments of his life, and he continued, "You know what! Whenever I am alone, I just think about her, trying to remember every moment from the beginning of our marriage till the last moments I have spent with her. Sometimes, it really amazes me that I have such feelings for her. Though words could have missed describing the times I have spent with her, a smile always appears on my face and it remains there. It always gives me time to think about the mistakes I made or the times I hurt her. It also lets me think of ways to please her, to make her happy."

"I feel I was their biggest mistake. I have tried to make them understand that they should think about me too, but they never bother. They never paid heed towards me, and that made me feel so lonely even in a crowd. Even though I possess every materialistic pleasure in this world, I find those things useless. Without the kind of love you just talked about, everything is useless. So, I left home to spend some moments in peace."

"Oh, then where are you headed?"

"I don't know. Will think about it after reaching Delhi. But honestly speaking, at first it seemed like I had made a wrong decision. But now, after talking to you, I am sure I should find out more about love and be happy. Maybe I am deriving too much from one bad relationship that I have seen."

"Hmm, sometimes being alone works. Loneliness is necessary. Solitude, to be more precise. But you can always use your loneliness as solitude. You just need to create a peaceful and happy environment around you. Like your very own personal world."

"Wow! Did you read all that in the book?" His glance and mine went to the book he had been reading, which now lay on one side. He only smiled, so I added, "Well, I have told you so much about me, but don't know anything about you. Did you also board from Varanasi? I gather, because you were the only one awake in the whole coach."

"Good guess! I boarded from Varanasi, a few minutes before you. I had some urgent work there," he said, smiling. Then almost suddenly, his smile faded and a hesitation crept in. "Well, you are not aware of where you wish to go. So, instead of roaming about here and there, you could come with me."

I was stunned. This man had to be really positive to be asking a stranger to come with him. The other way round as well. He seemed like a nice person but what if...?

"That's so kind of you to offer, but I don't want to trouble you anymore," I quickly answered.

"Trouble? No, it's no trouble. I am on vacation for a week. It would be great to spend time with you. I too have been alone for a few days, so I will feel happy if you accompany me."

"How alone? You said you live with your wife, right?"

"Yeah, but she has gone to her parents' home for a few days," he said, without elaborating. Taking my silence as agreement, he added, "Young man, this train will reach Delhi tomorrow. Then we will spend a night in my flat there, and then next morning, we will head towards Dehradun."

I took time in replying as I was left wondering about Dehradun, but before I could ask anything, he added, "Have you ever been to Dehradun?"

"No, never."

"Then you must visit. It is a lovely place, lush, great weather. I am sure you will find it very charming and peaceful. I visit this place almost every year."

"But where will we stay?" I asked.

"Aah, don't worry about that. I have a small cottage there. My wife loved the place, so I brought a small cottage there, so that whenever we visit Dehradun, we could live there."

"That's really cool. Okay, fine. I am ready to go." My face beamed, imagining the prospect of this journey. Though the conversation was quite interesting, I couldn't listen anymore for I felt sleepy. I didn't know when but I dozed off soon after.

When I woke up, the person was reading the same novel.

"Sorry, I fell asleep," I said, when our eyes met.

"No, its fine. You seemed tired. I also fell asleep after you," he said, smiled.

"Where are we? I guess we are about to reach," I said, looking out of the window.

"I don't where we are exactly. But a few minutes ago, I had asked the pantry guy and he had said that the train is running on time. If he is right, then we will reach in two more hours," he said.

That's when I suddenly realized that I didn't even know his name. I knew it had been quite late and would be embarrassing to introduce myself now. I was still pondering over this when his voice broke my concentration.

"See, we have been talking since last night and we don't know each other's names. Let me start. I am Randhir Sareen and I am a banker."

I smiled at his having read my thoughts and said, "I am Akshat Diwan."

6

A New Dawn

It was a wonderful evening when we stepped out onto the platform. There was a gentle breeze. I also realised how true the saying "the best way to get an idea of India's population is to see the railway platforms" stands. The Delhi station was crammed with people – old, young, crying children, young ones, and adults, men and women. Some came to see off someone, some came to board trains. Even before the train stopped, people on platforms were jumping onto the train, scrambling for seats. I saw that my friend had somehow dragged out his trolley bag.

"I really hate travelling with luggage," he said, trying to drag it as it got stuck. "The worst is carrying luggage while travelling in trains. I can't afford this torture."

"True," I said, "I think so too."

"I was not in the mood to carry the trolley bag and was packing my backpack, but my wife, after some arguing, packed my important stuff and clothes in this trolley bag. But luckily, when I opened the bag in Varanasi, I came to know that there were so many things in it that I'd require."

We stepped out of the station. And like everyone else, the first thing we faced was the jostling of auto drivers as they tried to secure passengers. I was baffled; nobody did that at airports.

I refused to move a step ahead when encountered with the auto drivers. To our surprise, one of them started snatching my bag, and my friend's trolley to secure me as his passenger, but I wasn't in the mood to take an auto.

Mr. Randhir said to me, "I know how they loot everyone, especially people visiting the city for the first time." I sniggered at their actions. They all asked in the same tone, "Where to, sir?"

He slowly said to me, "Let me show you how to work through such a situation. For future." And he winked.

So, just for that, my friend casually said, "Vasant kunj."

"No worries, only 300."

He said quietly to me, "If they ask for more than a hundred bucks, it means the place is not so near the station." I was astonished by the logic; this was new to me.

He nudged me and said, "Let's take the bus." He shook his head, rejecting the requests to take an auto. Some of the drivers left without saying much but few were still adamant, and started haggling with us.

"280 sir."

"275." Someone from my left shouted and started walking to the auto, as if he had offered me the best deal and that it was decided that I will take his auto. But when I didn't move an inch, he stopped near his auto.

"Ok. Final rate sir, 260. You know, we have to take u-turns, and there is a lot of traffic. This is the final rate," shouted one with a long beard, who looked like a beast rather than an auto driver.

Without saying anything to them, we moved, making our way away from them. When they saw that we were not interested, they also moved ahead, leaving us and moving towards another jet of passengers coming out of the railway station.

We moved to the bus stop, and checked out the bus details.

There were several people at the bus stop, waiting for their buses. Mr. Randhir said pointing towards an approaching bus, "The bus is coming."

Within a few seconds, the bus stopped. Luckily, it was not full when we boarded so we got seats. The bus was filled with people soon after.

When the bus was almost full, the driver turned around, checked the empty seats, waited for a few more seconds, then looking outside the bus, he shouted, "Vasant kunj, Vasant kunj." But when no one showed interest, the conductor stepped inside, told the driver to move and started asking us to pay for our tickets.

The bus started with a jerk, engine roared and sped off, but intermittently stopped due to traffic jams. The bus moved callously on the roads, not caring for the many pedestrians. My heart raced when I saw a boy get spared his life by an inch.

I wondered at the speed with which the bus moved, and the carelessness shown by the driver. I remembered what one of my friends said about Delhi buses and their drivers: the drivers used to be pilots first, habituated to 3d driving. But since they are now forced to drive in a 2d space, they don't have control over their driving. How I used to laugh at that joke!

I looked outside.

My eyes found beauty beyond expectations in huge hoardings, colourful posters, decorated shopping malls and clean roads. Commonwealth games had changed the face of Delhi from a dirty, crowded city to a beautiful, well-managed and clean city. The haphazard slouch of neglected buildings, small tenements had been thrashed away and there stood modern, lavish hotels, buildings, malls, shopping complexes attracting a wide variety of customers.

Soon, we reached Vasant kunj.

A security guard was at the entrance; seeing my friend, he saluted politely. My friend responded in the same way. We took the elevator up to the fourth floor and I followed him till he stopped in front of a door. I saw the name plate outside house number 4S. He inserted the key and the door opened with a sound of a click. We entered.

"This is my apartment," he said, keeping the bag on the other side. "Feel at home." And then he looked at me. I couldn't say or do anything, except smile. I was awestruck at his generosity. I glanced around the apartment with measuring eyes. To the door's right was a living room, connecting to the bathroom. Beyond that two rooms. The furniture looked quite new and was elegantly crafted. A sofa, a huge TV adorned the living room, with small vases kept beside the sofa. The walls had classic paintings, and there was a split AC on top. Overall, it looked beautiful.

"At that corner is the kitchen. If you need anything, you can go in and help yourself without hesitation," he said, and then he moved towards the bathroom. "Get freshened up. Then we will order some food, and then take a nap. Train journeys are tiring. Once rested and fresh, we could go out in the evening."

"Sure, thanks."

I came to the window, opened it and looked outside. Situated in a residential area, the house was surrounded by buildings on one side, and a street displaying small shops on the other.

After a short nap, we decided to go out for dinner. We walked, enjoying the evening. It was nippy. There were times a chill ran down my spine, sometimes I shivered. We walked past the houses and strolled towards the road, lit up by the yellow street lights. I was following my friend, since I was pretty new to the city. We strolled around, advanced to the street and moved onto several alleys, in search of a good Punjabi *dhaba*. Considering it was supper-time, the streets and roads were crammed with people and vehicles, and the air was filled with the sound of horns and other noise. The wide and brightly-lit street gave me the thrill of being in a big city, and I found it interesting to stroll aimlessly.

We walked on the pavement, looking around. At a distance, I saw a crowd of people gathered around a small stall for snacks and fast food. I thought about going for snack but then, I saw a chain of good restaurants and a small dhaba on the opposite side of the road. We walked on to see better restaurants that announced themselves through glittering lights and nicely painted boards unlike snack stalls.

My eyes lit up looking at a Punjabi dhaba. I had heard a lot about a dhaba at college and their cheap but scrumptious food. We ate at the dhaba, and the food was indeed as delicious as my friends had told me.

We returned to the room an hour later. The fatigue from the journey caused sleep to settle over my eyes. When Mr. Randhir saw my tiredness, he said, "I guess you are feeling sleepy. I am also tired. I guess we should retire for the night."

"Yeah," I nodded. But since I didn't know where to sleep for the night, I waited him to tell me.

"You can sleep over there, if you don't have any problem," he said, indicating towards the corner of the living room where O saw a single bed placed.

"Yeah, sure. No problem. It's totally fine," I said.

"Do you need anything? Perhaps a bed sheet or something to cover yourself up?" he asked me before leaving the living room.

"No, it's totally cool. I don't think I need anything."

It usually took me some time to settle into a strange bed. However, that night, within a few minutes, I was in the lap of deep sleep. As I had slept off early, I woke up very early the next morning. It was still dark, and the room was comfortably cold. I didn't care to come out of the bed. Since I had nothing to do, I tried to sleep again. When I realised I could not, my mind started planning for the day ahead of me. I thought we would leave for Dehradun, but I heard my friend speaking to someone over phone.

"Okay, in an hour, I will be there." And he put the phone down.

I heard his footsteps approaching in my direction. I turned around to see him; he looked relieved to see me awake and said, "Hey Akshat! Good morning. Did you sleep well?"

I smiled and nodded. I could not hold back and asked him about the phone call. "I have to go to office. Though I am on leave, some urgent work has come up now. I will be back in the evening. We will leave for Dehradun tomorrow morning then. I hope that's okay with you," he said, as he wore his shirt.

"Why don't you go around Delhi? Go and see the city. It will be good for you," he continued.

"That sounds good to me. I was planning to do just that. But I need to inform my father about my whereabouts before that," I said.

"Yeah, that would be good. There is a place right at the end of the street where you can do that. Oh, do you have money with you? Because I might be late. So you have your lunch and dinner where you please."

"Thank you so much; I have cash. Don't worry about me. I will go around and see Delhi in a while. You are leaving right away?"

"Yes. Oh and you can use my computer if you wish to. There," he said, pointing to the corner of his room. "No password."

"Okay, I am getting late. You know this investment banking job. I would never suggest you take up this job. Lots of tension! And in return, you get a fat salary to buy medicines to reduce that same tension." He said in an amusing way and we laughed. Then, he quickly wore his shoes and left. Just at the door, he looked around and told me where he had kept the key to the main door in case I wanted to go out.

After he left, I did just that. I browsed on the Internet the major tourist spots in Delhi and made a list. I made notes, and collected every piece of information about travelling around the city.

I finally went out with a list of tourist places I wanted to visit. Lots of stories and praise, sometimes exaggerated, sometimes genuine and sometimes realistic always made me curious to visit these places.

Though the sky was overcast, it did not show any trace of rain. After some misunderstanding in taking the right bus and some brief arguments with the conductors and drivers, I finally reached the Lotus Temple. The clouds had shifted in a pattern behind the temple, and the sun rays were falling directly on it, clearly making a silhouette of one of most beautiful temples. It illuminated the structure in a way that I couldn't help saying, "This is just beautiful". I was awestruck even to react, or blink. The surrounding was green, and a well-maintained garden added a new charm to it. Though the praying hall inside was huge, and voices of the tourists were echoing all around me, I still felt a deep sense of peace. A few things of the past few days came back to me, but I pushed them to the background again.

Once I moved out of there, I spent some time at Red Fort, ate street food at Chandni Chowk, went to India Gate for a stroll up to the President's house and finally came back to Vasant Kunj. There was a lot more to be seen in the city, but I had carefully selected these few places to be able to look around without rushing.

I reached my friend's house by half past seven. I had just freshened up and settled when he came back at around 8. He held several plastic bags.

"Hi, how was your day? I hope it wasn't boring. I am sorry for having left you to yourself," he said, keeping the bags on the table.

"No, it was great," I replied.

"Really? I know you weren't home because I had called from office once. Nobody answered; I assumed you were out."

"Yeah, I visited several places today. It was kind of fun and exciting. How did your work go?" I asked.

"Oh, it went as usual – boring and exhausting," he said. "By the way, I have brought food for us. Can you plate it on the dining table? I will just change, get freshened up, and then we will eat," he said, and headed towards the bathroom.

"Yeah, sure," I said, and got off the sofa. I was happy to be able to help the man who was doing so much for a stranger. He didn't know me, had no clue where I was from, for all he knew I could have been a crook. But he seemed like a kind soul. Moreover, he had shown more care for me than my father ever had in the past years.

I went over to the table and checked that plastic bags. It had a lot of food. Pulao, chicken, paneer, naans and salad. I thought it was excessive For two people, but I set the table.

As he came out of bathroom after changing, we started our dinner together.

"So, where all did you go today?" he asked.

"Oh I went to the Lotus Temple, and then the Red Fort, and India Gate. I even had some street food at Chandni Chowk." I was really excited. "Although I couldn't spend much time at each place, they sure are beautiful," I said. "Your house is also very good. I wonder how you got it."

"Means?" He sounded confused, and his facial expression reflected that.

"You said that you got transferred here. In cities like Delhi, if I am right, it is not so easy to find good houses?"

"Yeah, right. When I got transferred here, I was living in a rented flat. Within one month, I started feeling lonely. Nothing to do except going to office and coming home. I started missing my wife."

"So, you didn't come here with your wife at the time of transfer?"

"No. I hadn't made any arrangement for a house. And it's so difficult to settle down in this city."

"That's true...But, this apartment is really nice," I said. When I heard the word "missing", I realized that I was also missing Naina, perhaps for the first time. I saw that we were almost done with dinner. It was really delicious, I remarked.

"Why don't you take some more naan? You have hardly eaten a thing," he said, looking at my empty plate. "All this food is just for us."

"Yes, I will take some more. I just got engrossed in listening to you," I said and smiled. "What happened after that? When did you get your wife here?"

"I will let you know at the appropriate time."

After finishing the food, we came to the living room and switched the TV on. I had the remote and kept surfing through to find something interesting, but there was nothing good.

"When I visited here, I observed one funny thing," he said. I saw a smile creep across over his lips. I reduced the volume on the TV.

"And what was that?"

"When I had discussed with my friends that people in big cities don't even know their neighbours, in spite of living next door for years, I understood how busy life was for everyone here. And I realized how it is important to understand that if someone is giving you time, you should also respect theirs."

When he was done speaking, I contemplated over his words. He was absolutely right. And this was the first time I realized something: I remembered how much importance and time Naina gave me. I felt the slow stirrings of guilt within me.

"*Arey*, I forget to tell you one thing," he said, "I have called for a cab. He will be here tomorrow morning."

"That's good. What time?" I asked.

"Around 6 or 7 a.m. I think we should sleep now, or it would be too difficult to wake up in the morning," he said, switching off the TV.

"You can make yourself comfortable. Goodnight," he said and left the room.

"Good night. I would like to know something that has really made me curious," I put hesitantly, adjusting my pillow.

"And what is that?"

"Actually, when we were coming home, you preferred taking a bus rather than an auto. I think money is not a problem for you. You have such a big house and very good lifestyle," I asked.

He smiled before replying to my question. "Yeah, you are right. I could have given the person three hundred rupees, without bargaining, but tell me something! If I can reach my destination in just ten rupees, why do I pay three hundred! I have seen the importance of money, so I don't want to waste it on useless things."

"That's very true."

"Can we now get some sleep?" I nodded and he switched off the light before leaving the room.

7

To the Doon Valley

Next morning, as the sky was beginning to display hues of red, we decided to leave Delhi for Dehradun. I awoke early, freshened up and got my backpack ready.

The taxi that Mr. Randhir had booked had come. After a few words with the driver, we sat comfortably in the backseat. For about five hours from starting, the journey was smooth; but for the last half-an-hour or so, the journey turned to curvaceous. The route was tremendously complicated because of the hilly region. We went up the hill and down, along the narrow road where there was barely enough room to squeeze past other vehicles. There were numerous curves and turns, but I enjoyed the drive. In fact, the greenery all around was beautiful. After about fifteen more minutes, we stopped outside a house. It seemed that we had reached our destination. I stepped out of the taxi and looked around: large mountains, green surroundings imbued with a vernal freshness. The air was startlingly fresh and the silence that filled the surroundings too profound. The sky appeared perfectly blue with silver flecks of clouds soaring upward. The mixture of the warmth of sunlight and the chillness of wind was giving a gentle feeling to the mind and senses. The valley was echoing with the chirping of birds, but I couldn't see them anywhere. I was so engrossed that I wanted to feel everything about the place within this short period of time. It was so calm, so pleasing.

"Shall we go?" he asked.

"Sure," I turned around. He was smiling at me, at my relaxed face.

We walked a few yards before we stopped before the small wooden house. The trees and bushes in front were beautifully trimmed. He walked past me, turned the knob and opened the door: It opened with a creaking sound. I followed him and stepped inside, into the living room. As we entered the room, a dusty smell immediately struck me and I coughed. I could see that the penetrating odours assailed his memory, made him remember something unforgettable. As he entered the room, the smell struck him too and he winced. A look of grief came over his face. Panic took over him and eyes stared into the vacuum of a room, looking for something; I couldn't guess what at that time. The wooden floor echoed with his footsteps. I moved towards the window, and there was revealed the panoramic view of mountains, and the valley at the distance. It was a marvellous view. Shifting my look from the mountains to the room, I found that the room was almost barren and there were hardly any adornments. In the name of furniture, there were a few easy chairs, a sofa and an old dining table in the corner, all covered with plastic sheets. On the other side of the wall, there was a large, open-style fireplace but it showed no sign of having contained a fire recently. Considering it was a hill station, the room was chilly. For many months, it seemed as if the room had passed without any visitor.

Silence hung over us and neither of us made any attempt to break it. But my intuition spoke something about silence. The silence seemed so closely attached with that person, telling me something different every time I saw his face. It was not normal, for his muscles were twisted in a sort of invisible sorrow that I couldn't interpret at that time.

Keeping my bag on nearby chair, I looked out the window, but turned around when he spoke.

"Sorry, needs cleaning up," he said and started taking out the plastic sheets.

"Yes, it seems no one has visited for a long time," I walked towards him and helped him in uncovering the furniture.

"Yes, I am visiting after exactly a year. Generally, apart from me, no one visits here," he said, keeping his eyes on his work.

"Oh, that's why! But why a whole year? You and your wife can visit sometime in between," I asked in a questioning tone.

"No…" his tone was quite soft.

When he didn't reply, I didn't think it necessary to ask anything else. "Is there a broom around here?"

"There," he pointed with his finger. It was behind the door. I started sweeping the floor. It was the first time that I was doing this. Surprisingly, I didn't find it an uncomfortable task.

Soon, we cleaned the room together, made out the bed and adjusted the table.

"I am starving. You must be too. Let me order something for us. We will have lunch, then take some rest. In the evening, we will go for a walk around the city. It's lovely," he said, in a single breath.

"Yeah, sure. But from where will you order the food?" I asked.

"Aah! Don't worry about that. I know a hotel nearby who delivers food. Let me call them," he said, and moved aside to make the call.

Within half-an-hour or so, the hotel delivered the food. We had our lunch. I must say, the food was tasty and it was eaten along with some witty conversation, which I enjoyed immensely.

Being tired of the long drive, we dozed off soon after. It was already evening when I woke up. I saw Mr. Randhir sitting by the window, looking outside.

When he saw me coming out of the bed, he said, "Hope you had good rest."

"Yeah, but did you rest? You seem to have been awake for quite long."

"No, I just woke up. Perhaps ten minutes ago."

After a prolonged silence, he asked in a polite tone, "Shall we go for walk around the streets?"

"Yeah, just give me two minutes," I moved towards the washbasin, splashed water on my face. The water was a bit cold, got me out of my drowsiness completely.

We walked out of the cottage, strolled towards the other street. It was lovely, echoing with the chirping of birds and the quiet charm of the woods, both really peaceful to my senses.

"This place is really very beautiful," I said to him.

"Yeah, indeed. Soothing and charming."

We kept strolling till the velvet of the cloudless sky grew darker and the stars became brighter. After that we returned to the cottage. He lit the fireplace.

There was nothing particular to do, so I simply sat on the sofa and enjoyed the warmth of the fire. While on our way back, my new friend had bought a newspaper to keep track of the share market, and he was reading that. Few times, he raised his eyes from the paper to look at me and a few times, our eyes met. I smiled in return.

"Sir, you were saying something in the train, but I had slept, so I could not get what you were saying." I made an attempt to initiate a conversation.

"Sir? Please call me Randhir."

"How can I? You are quite elder to me. You're like my big brother."

"Then *bhaiya* would be fine. Isn't it?" he said.

"Yeah, that would be fine." I smiled.

"Now tell me what you were saying."

"You were going to tell me how you both met," I told him after remembering.

"Yeah, right."

"The joy on your face when you spoke about her on the train, I think you two are meant for each other. Isn't it really nice," I said, folding my legs on the seat of the sofa.

He smiled wistfully. But he didn't utter a word. It seemed that he was lost for a moment. He regained his consciousness and said with a smile, "Yes, we are. But we had to work at it. We had our tough times understanding each other."

"In understanding each other? You had an arranged marriage?" I asked, surprised. "I thought you both had a love marriage and initially it might have been tough for you to begin all those things. I meant in understanding each other, knowing each other's likes or dislikes."

He laughed before he replied, "Yes, we had an arranged marriage and I met her first only on the day I went with my parents to see the girl."

"You married a girl whom you met for the first time in your 25 years of existence. That's really cool. It would have been really tough."

"Yes, but I love those moments."

"You know, my parents had a love marriage but it seems like now that the love they had has just vanished."

"I sympathize with you," he made a remark. "In my case, everything turned out in a way that I had never imagined."

Hearing all this things from his mouth filled me with sudden surge of curiosity to know about him. To my surprise, I noticed that this excitement made me realize for the first time that I wasn't worried much about home, but was rather excited about my friend's life.

"How did it all begin? I would love to know."

He stood and walked towards the fireplace. I watched him. He threw some more logs into the fire, and then returned to the sofa.

"There are so many memories, so many; I can't begin to describe them! They were wonderful times, the times between us, how we lived wonderful lives, the best kind of lives you can imagine, not like today's generation, though the difference is not in time but in our approach."

Soon he was lost in his memories. The panorama of his life was unrolling before me. It filled me with a deep curiosity as I had never felt this close to anyone.

PART 2

8

His-story

At some point in life, there comes a time when almost everyone has to get married and I believe this is very natural. Everyone has to make up their mind to move in with a stranger, even in love marriages. There are many aspects of a person that you end up exploring with the passage of time. Looking back at those years, when I was forced to marry, I feel strange. Back then, I had felt a sudden sense of uneasiness when my parents had talked to me about the marriage for the first time. I was certainly not ready for that but sometimes, in life, it so happens that you have to do things you don't wish to.

Well to begin with, I never gave any thought to such things. Too busy for this. But now when I think about it, it surprises me. Several things changed over this period of time. It would not be wrong to mention that I started living in real after I married her and I never gave any thought to what would have happened had I married someone else.

When I started reaching the age of marriage, my parents began looking for a bride for me. I would think about my marriage intermittently - at times with excitement for I had heard from my colleagues that life changes after marriage, that it is the most important stage of life; at other times with dread, about how a person like me was going to handle things after marriage? Living with a stranger for a long part of my life sometimes sent a shiver through my body, and I tried deciphering every aspect of this.

Before marriage, certainly my life followed a routine, and there was no unnecessary excitement. I woke up, ate breakfast, went for work, came back, completed my work and slept. Nothing adventurous really happened.

But one day, as I can recall, on 25th August, I arrived home as usual and was delightfully surprised at the happy mood and radiant faces of my parents. Papa was dressed in a suit and tie. My mother was also dressed well; she wore an expensive sari and jewellery too.

They were smiling. I also greeted them happily as I kept my office bag on the bed and loosened my tie. "Seems like you are going to a marriage or reception party. Is it?"

"Yes, for a marriage," my father replied back.

"Oh, great! Where? I didn't see any invitation card."

Going to any marriage clearly brought out a grand mood in them, I knew. But their deceptive smiles didn't convey anything more to me. I cast a suspicious glance over to them, "Where?"

"To your wedding," my mother said. "Our neighbour Sharma ji told us about a girl; she lives on the other side of this city. He was saying that they are nice people and their daughter is homely, religious and well-educated."

Listening to my mother's word, in an instant, all my fatigue left me and I gave them a puzzled look which didn't bother them at all.

"Oh god!" I shrugged, "So again you want me to get ready and go there with you?"

Both nodded at the same time.

It was the fourth time that I was getting ready to see a girl. The last three occasions had been quite bitter and funny. So, this time too, I didn't give much consideration and quietly got ready.

While combing my hair, my mother shouted, "The girl's photo is on the dressing table… it's kept in an envelope. You can check it out."

I didn't reply. After getting ready, I went into the room. There was a medium sized envelope kept on the dress table. Like every time, with butterflies in my stomach, I wondered this time too about how the girl would turn out to be. I pulled the photo out of envelope and cast a glance over the photo. She looked good; but I had no special way of looking at or interpreting people at that time so I couldn't interpret much about her. However, unlike other times, this time my heart filled with some expectation about this meeting. I didn't know why. Might be the innocence that was on her face, or perhaps her pleasant, homely look. I wasn't certain of anything.

"Did you pray to god for good luck?" Mummy asked when I came out of the room.

"Mummy, you know very well that I don't believe in god," I tried to remind her again.

"No, betaji. You must not say that, at least not on such auspicious occasions," Mummy tried to convince me.

"Okay," I went into the pooja room. Without much ado, I came out within a minute.

"Your prayer is done?" Mummy was surprised at how quick I was.

"No, shall I start a havan? Spend a few days on it?" I asked in an irritated voice. "Yes, I prayed to god, asked that he should give a good *bahu* for my mother."

Listening to this, papa burst into laughter. I eventually joined in and Mummy frowned.

I don't remember when I renounced my faith over god and lost my belief in old religious views. Whatever it might be, it was like even if I reached a stage of utter grief and hopelessness, my views towards God would remain unaltered. I would never ask or say anything to god, to the creator of this universe.

Initially, I remember, it was neither that I had renounced my faith over god completely nor did I have complete trust over him. But a situation came when I saw that even after my mother's true and sincere worship and her dedication and devotion towards god, he couldn't rectify any of my family problems. We only suffered. I finally renounced my faith over god and formed just one belief: a belief in myself, that it's my life and I am the architect of my life. I came to believe that worshipping god or someone whose existence is unsure, is completely useless. But I never came in the way of my mother's belief. Sometimes, I talked to god, not on my part, rather on behalf of my mother, when I saw utter despair in the hearts of my family members. At a time when my father didn't get salary for seven consecutive months and all of us were in great many problems. But what I said to God through my grief and angry sobs was something like this: "Hey, god. Why are you sometimes… no, not sometimes… every single time… so cruel to us. My mother worships you, so sincerely and always chants your prayers but you don't listen to her and always leave her and her family in such grief. You can see our situation. How we are spending our life in such penury. At this moment, I know I am helpless, so I am speaking to you… but I will make sure that in the future, I will take care of my parents and give them a luxurious life. Please do something, please do something." I don't know how many times I have begged. And as expected, the crying resulted in nothing, and my tears dried off, turned into cursing the god for making people live in an illusion. But I was completely out of this illusion, and soon after, quite abruptly, I was not crying anymore. In fact, I grew harder and harder. The pathetic situation completely vacuumed out of me but learning from the situation, I completely pulled out of it, and made myself strong enough to endure all types of problems.

But I never knew that there will be time when I will have to ask something from god.

Anyway, coming back to the evening I was going to see the girl: no one asked me whether I liked the girl in the photo, nor did I tell them.

We reached Mr. Sinha's home in half an hour. My neighbour, Mr. Sharma also accompanied us. He knew Mr. Sinha was far better at making conversation than my family was. The Sinhas were at the front gate, and it looked like they were waiting for us. After exchanging initial pleasantries, we were taken to the dining room. The house wasn't very big. I didn't think much about this as my home was also not big.

I was sitting silently on one side of the sofa, feeling uneasy. My father was busy in talking with Mr. Sinha and my mother to Mrs. Sinha. Looking at their demeanour, I sensed them as simple, honest people. When little time passed, to be honest, my eyes started searching for her.

"Sareen ji lives in Bihar from the very beginning, like you," Sharma uncle said. "And our Ramesh ji is also from Bihar."

"*Wah*, that's good," My father said. Mr. Sinha was a bit silent and submissive probably because he was the father of girl.

"Why are you not having some snacks and sweets?" he said, offering the plates to me and papa.

"*Uff,* Sinhaji, why are you bothering for this? Why don't you talk to Akshat, my son?" Papa said. He sometimes acted over-excitedly.

Mr. Sinha nodded and sat beside me. I looked at him and smiled.

"Sharma ji was telling me that you work in a bank," he asked, quite politely.

"Yes, I work as a bank manager in State Bank of India." My reply was also polite. He asked me a few more question and I replied accordingly. I inferred that he too felt quite uneasy in asking questions. Looking at his words, behaviour and tone, I easily understood that he too was a kind hearted and honest person like my father.

"Sinha ji, we would love to see your daughter. What do you say Gitika?" my father said.

"Yes, of course." My mother added.

"Sure, why not? Radha, call our daughter," Mr. Sharma smiled at us, and directed his wife to call their daughter. She left the room and walked towards the bedroom.

When she arrived from the room, my eyes were fixed on her. She was in a pink sari, with her *aanchal* drawn over her head. Her eyes were downcast, and she walked slowly, feeling shy. She had a graceful length of limb and fall of shoulder. She was accompanied by her mother on one side, who held her one hand, and on the other side by a girl, almost of her age. Might be her friend, I thought. Initially, when I raised my eyes, it never crossed my mind that it was to be the girl whom I was going to marry.

"Here is my daughter, Radhika," Mr. Sinha said. She sat beside her mother.

"Oh, such a beautiful name," my mother said. She was the first to talk to Radhika. Then papa followed suit. They kept talking, and I kept wondering what was I supposed to do!

When everyone had finished their share of talking, my father turned towards Mr. Sinha and said, "Sinha ji, we have all met Radhika. If you permit, let Radhika and Akshat get to know each other. Moreover, they are the ones who have to decide."

"Sure. Why not! Priyanka, please," he said to Radhika's friend.

"Yes, uncle?" she was happy to help, it seemed.

"Beta, they want to talk. Please guide him and Radhika to the room."

"Sure," then we both headed towards the room.

While going towards the room, I was in a quandary about what I would ask her. When we were left alone, I felt some restlessness within me. Though I had met three girls earlier, in those instances, the conversation hadn't gone beyond the parents. So I had never been in this state of mind. This was the first time that I was talking to a woman I could get married to.

Once we were in the room, Priyanka left, giving us the privacy we'd need. I looked around the room. It was better decorated than the dining room. The bed had a vibrant new and clean sheet, the window was draped in beautiful curtains, there were two sofa-type chairs right next to the bed and the walls were adorned with several paintings.

Both of us were waiting for the other to initiate something, but when she didn't say any word, I asked her politely, "Please sit." She accepted my request gracefully and sat down. I too sat on the other chair.

When nothing seemed appropriate to say, I chose to remain silent, patiently waiting for her to say something. After a brief pause, I initiated the conversation. I didn't know whether it was right or not, I started speaking what I was feeling at time. "You know, I was not aware of this marriage proposal and came to know about it just a few hours ago. I don't know what to talk about at this moment. Our parents have decided for our future and we are meant to take the decision for the next step."

She nodded mutely, keeping her eyes down. I glanced at her. Her eyes were hazy and her beauty was softened by an air of nervousness and uneasiness. Her face was serene though, devoid of any agitation, like a swan swimming in the pond. It looks so calm from the outside but beneath the water, a swan relentlessly peddles. It must have been the same for her too; I guessed that she beautifully masked her tension.

I was so involved in my words while speaking, that I forgot that I was talking to someone with whom I might spend rest of my life, would sleep on the same bed with and would have to share the smallest of things with, but when I realized this, I stopped my conversation abruptly, and this propelled her to ask, "Why have you stopped speaking?"

This surprised me.

I continued. "I never had much thought about marriage, as I have devoted my life to fulfilling my parents' dreams. I completed my graduation and applied for a job at the bank. Luckily, I got selected and now, I am a bank manager. I don't know why I feel like saying this to you. Never said such things to anyone before. And, honestly, I don't know whether I have any good qualities or not, but I never tried smoking and drinking."

Radhika, surprising me, showed a gleam of interest in her eyes and listened to me carefully before I stopped again. "I am so sorry. I don't know. I am singing my own song rather than listening to you. Honestly speaking, I don't know why I have shared all this with you. Have never done this earlier."

She smiled over this 'but' again, still didn't say anything on her own. When she didn't initiate saying anything, I tried to bluff about her interests. "I was told that you like cooking and painting. Are those paintings on the wall done by you?"

"Yes. I did those paintings," she said, still keeping her eyes down. Her voice was soft.

"These are really great. I have never seen such beautiful paintings before. I have tried sketching but couldn't sketch more than simple triangular mountains and the rising sun between them," she smiled, but suppressed it immediately.

"I am a non-believer of god. Do you believe in god?" I asked.

"Hmm," she made a very short reply.

"I always say to my mom that it is just my own opinion that I don't believe in god but I never interfere with others' beliefs," I said. "You have no questions for me at all? You can ask anything without hesitation. I believe it is very important to talk."

For the first time, she raised her eyes, looked at me and smiled, "No, it's fine." As she stopped, her mother knocked the door.

"Conversation over?" she asked.

I was about to say no, but before I could, Radhika nodded in a positive way. It really surprised me. She hadn't asked me anything so far. I didn't have any clue about how she had judged me or if she had rejected me based on my talkative behaviour.

"That's good," her mother walked to her. I also stood up and walked out of room. Seeing me, my mother walked towards me and asked me, "Is that a yes?"

Even after talking to her alone, I couldn't know much about her except for a few things. I came to know a whole lot of things from my parents, though. Her father was professor in the arts college and her mother was a housewife. Both were very religious.

So she also grew up to be devout. Every morning, she woke up listening to the chanting of prayers. Though her house was not that big, it had all the required facility: enough, but not as much as I have today. Since her father was a professor, she also grew up with the habit of reading books, and she read a lot of books.

I remembered. I had seen a book shelf piled with lots of books in one corner of the room. Some of the books seemed yellowish and torn but were kept safely.

I couldn't react in a way that might confirm my decision. But one night, I nodded in positive way when my mother kept asking me. She called Radhika's home to know what she had said. To my surprise, she too had given the positive signal towards this alliance.

9

In Retrospect

I did not interfere while he was talking. I just heard him speak his heart out. A smile came over him every time he talked of Radhika. I stared directly at him, looked at him with perplexed eyes. A moment later, he broke the silence and asked me:

What happened after that, you wonder?

An auspicious date was finalized. Our *kundalis* were matched. Though I did not believe in all this too much, it was still overwhelming to listen that we were a perfect match and our nakshstras matched perfectly well.

Soon, the day of the wedding arrived. We had barely talked during the days between the first meeting and the marriage. We met once or twice, but that's about it. The time of preparing for the wedding passed with a pace that suggested that time had wings. Several things had to be arranged. Shopping. Arrangement for the guests. Just a few days before the marriage, relatives started visiting one by one.

And finally, our wedding day arrived.

On the wedding day, it was bedlam at my house. Looking at the energy of the relatives, I felt something that I had never felt before. I woke up amid the talking and noise. Every relative of mine was hovering around me all the time, never left me for a single moment alone, forcing me to perform all kind of rituals. If I sit and count now, I could say that I had to perform some ten-fifteen odd rituals. Or maybe more. I hopelessly looked at my mother, who was the happiest person on the earth at that time. Every time I was furious at the relatives and looked at my mother for redemption, she gave me a flying kiss in response. Beginning from the crack of dawn till noon, I was engaged in the rituals. It felt quite bizarre doing those rituals when love is the only ritual that should be performed all the time to strengthen any relationship. My father was also happy, but he kept himself away from the drama and was busy in the payment of bills. On the other side, the Band-Baja group was lurking around to see what was happening and was annoyed over this prolonged pooja. I heard them saying: "Sir, we have to go for another marriage too. Please be quick and clear our bills," in an impatient tone to my father.

"Just a few more minutes," Papa said. "You know that these things take time."

After fifteen minutes, I got dressed. My parents had bought me a *sherwani* for this occasion. A cream-colored one, embroidered greatly with different pearls and stones. It was quite beautiful. Without wasting any more time, I got ready to leave. My father also got ready. He wore a dark blue striped suit. This was the first time in his fifty years that he had worn a suit. I came to know that he wasn't ready to buy this suit, but because of my mom, he had bought it. When I came out of room, I saw him and smiled.

"Toh beta ji, how am I looking?" he said, struggling to knot the tie.

"It is not important how you are looking. You should ask how our son is looking," my mom chided him.

"Oh, he always looks nice. What's there to ask! Plus, it's our son's wedding. I have to look good too… otherwise what will our son's in-laws say about us. See, the son's father is so old and cranky," papa said in a jovial tone.

I laughed and came closer to him. "No, papa. You are looking too good in this suit! Like an officer. Let me tie this knot," Tying the knot, I looked at my mom. She too was in her best outfit, loaded with all the jewellery that she had bought and collected over a period of time. She never wore costly saris in general and it was only during these occasions that we witnessed her in such gorgeous attire.

The atmosphere grew intense with the passage of time. Everyone was shouting and chaotic. Even in such clamour, when it was impossible to identify a single tone out of the many being thrown across the house, I could recognize my *mausaji's* voice due to its familiarity, more because of the way in which he conveyed something to my *mausi*:

"Where is my belt? I can't find it. Sunita, are you listening?" He directed this at his wife, while looking at all others. She ran towards him with his belt.

"How many times have I told you to keep everything in order? It is too messy to find anything in your suitcase." He tried to bring down her voice. But mausiji was in her own spirits too.

"Have you ever tried to find anything? Everything is in front of your eyes and still you cannot see! Just shouting at me all the time like I am your maid or something," she said, but not in a tone that would hurt him.

Everyone began to laugh at this and just when my father said, "Don't scare the groom; he might say no to go" the room broke into a fresh round of laughter. Everyone was laughing, except me. No more jokes could be cracked because the band baja interrupted again.

"Sir, we are getting late."

"Okay, just two minutes more," I said.

He gave an annoyed look before standing aside in a submissive way, for he had no choice but to do that. From a distance I could hear him murmuring under his breath that he had been put into a cage today.

Amid this chaos, our *baraat* left for the marriage hall. The street wore an air of frenzy, the band happily produced a loud musical noise that roared through the atmosphere, forcing people to break free from their air of normalcy. The bumping bodies, swaying in excitement and in irregular patterns began to intensify with time near the car in which I was sitting. The car crawled at a snail's pace, and inside it I was feeling uneasy. Women were following the car, throwing petals, coins and other things, which hammered against the car roof. The tick-tick sound proliferated with time and I wondered at the number of scratches it would give my car.

Within one hour, we reached the girl's home. It seemed like all their family members were waiting for us. Bursting of crackers, the merry sounds and noises, the music, the whole environment was festive.

Soon, the pandit arrived and laid out his paraphernalia. On the day, I didn't feel anything against this rituals, mantras or shlokas that would be flowing out soon from his mouth. I was seated silently. He chanted some mantra and said, "Yajman, call the bride". After a few minutes, Radhika came slowly. I stole a glance in her direction. She was in a red bridal sari, embroidered with golden threads, her wedding dress decorated with different jewellery and the *pallu* was drawn over her head. Her eyes were downcast, as she had kept them when she had spoken to me for the first time.

In a few hours, all the rituals for the wedding got over and we walked around the fire seven times, taking an oath to support each other for the whole life. I didn't know that those seven circumambulations around the fire meant something. You know, Akshat, all of them really means something. Each one of them is a promise to make one's marriage successful. I realized its worth later.

Next day, we left for our home, taking my newly wedded wife.

To be precise, you know, at one point of time in everyone's life, someone coming into your life brings a wonderful change. Sometimes we don't recognize it in the first go, but realize it with the passage of time for sure. That's what happened to me when she pushed the little pot of rice and entered my home, and soon into my heart as well.

While he said this, I didn't know why, but Naina's face swayed across my mind again. So charming, so caring, with a genuine smile. Purity.

Things turned out in such a way that I couldn't touch her for a year. That first night of our wedding, when I entered the room, she had already slept. The *pallu*, which I had assumed would be drawn over her face, had slid a little bit, uncovering her face, but not completely. When I found her sleeping, I glanced over my watch. It was past midnight. She had slept waiting for me to come in. Before going to sleep, I stole a glance to the uncovered part of her face, couldn't gather my strength to draw the remaining part of the *pallu* aside and see her face completely. I smiled at her and slept. It was an uneasy feeling sleeping on the bed, next to her. And my uneasiness resulted into a one-hand distance between us.

Next morning, when I opened my eyes, I found no one on

the other side. When I came out, she had already bathed, was draped in a sari and was in the kitchen, cooking something sweet for our family.

I also joined my family in the drawing room, after freshening myself up. My parents were laughing at something, I was flipping the pages of the newspaper when Radhika came carrying the tray. That was the first time I saw her after the marriage. She looked more beautiful than ever before. Simple make up, the red vermillion, a red *bindi* between the two eyebrows gleamed. Lips coated with a light shade of lipstick. The hair was dancing like a snake on her back as it was still wet and she hadn't tied them up. I continued glancing at her till she came in front of me and our eyes met.

I cannot say that the first month of our marriage was entirely smooth or entirely bumpy. I knew it always takes time to make a perfect connection. Learning from the small things is the beginning of unconditional love. Initially, for a person like me, it was hardest to do something. Things like getting close to her, talking something romantic or telling her that I had started having feelings for her. Every feeling that was developed during the days secretly seemed like a magical chord that started striking your life. I remember when I saw my wife sitting on the sofa, wearing a gown, having come out of bathroom after taking a bath; it seemed like butterflies had spread across my heart and stomach. When she turned to me, cleaning her hair and drying them with a towel, I just averted my eyes in sheer shyness. Those are moments that marked the beginning of our closeness and whenever I remember those days, I just smile.

On such comments, I found myself unsure about how to respond and it always surprised me how others could see this, either in my expressions or body language.

When the clocks struck eleven, it was announced by eleven small gong sounds from the antique watch on the table. He looked at the watch, paused for a moment.

"Aah, it's 11. We should go to bed. I will continue the rest of the story tomorrow." I nodded, though my heart didn't allow. I was eager to know the rest of the story.

After he left the fireplace, and headed towards his room for sleep, I drowned myself in his words. How he would have felt at that time? What would it have been like for him to say these things to his own wife in such subtle rhythm? I tried to place myself in his place and imagined this, and that helped me forget about my home for a while: slowly, unconsciously my eyelids dropped in sleep. And a few times, the face of Naina hovered in front of me, and it brought something different within me. A feeling that I was missing her.

10

Alternate Realities

*N**ext day, we went around Dehradun, even visited a monastery on the outskirts of the city. The joy of being in a peaceful surrounding was unparalleled. When we sat in front of fireplace that evening, I was really excited to know what happed after that.*

He stood up, strolled towards the window and opened it. a cool breeze rushed into the room. I looked out the window while he returned and resumed the story from the same point where he had left it the previous night.

One morning, I received a letter. When I checked out, it turned out to be an appointment letter from HDFC bank for which I had applied a year back. I had lost all hope of hearing from them, and so I felt exaltation. But for that, I had to go to Delhi. They had offered me a job at the Delhi branch and at any cost, I didn't want to leave this opportunity.

Since I had no arrangement in Delhi, I left Radhika at home and arrived in Delhi. That was the first time I had visited the city.

Living in a rented house as a paying guest for two months, I found myself in such shambles of life and my solitariness grew over these months that started haunting. So I decided to move from here, and to call my parents and my wife to live with me. So I bought a flat in west Delhi, and for this, I had to search in the classified ads for builders and real estate dealers. My terms got fixed with some Mr. Sudhir Sharma, a broker. My parents were not ready to come here as papa still had a few years left before his retirement. Radhika came. I went with Radhika for the final approval of our home. Moreover, we had to live there, so she had to like it too. When I was dealing with the broker and owner, Radhika looked around. I saw her that she meticulously checked out every corner of the apartment. It was agreeable, spacious, properly airy and sun-filled. Well-painted, glossy and amazingly placed lights all around were giving it a pleasant look. It had three bedrooms and possessed the luxury of a spacious gallery. At last, she approved it. In the few days after that, I signed all the papers and bought the home on loan. I kept this as a surprise for my parents. But since they were not yet ready to come over, I had to tell them about it. I was a big achievement and my parents had to feel the joy.

"What! You have bought a flat there?" certainly, my mother's smile and surprise left me content. But before she could say more, papa snatched the phone from her and said in an ecstatic tone, "When did you buy it?"

"Just about a few days back."

'You didn't tell us anything. What about the money? How did you manage alone?"

"I wanted to surprise you all. That's why I was asking you to come here, and you kept refusing."

"Beta, I still have a few years of job left. After that, where will we go? We will just pack our bags and come to Delhi to live with you," Papa said jokingly.

It was my fiftieth day at the new office and Radhika's first day in Delhi. I arrived home at my regular hour, in the evening around 7:00 pm. She unlocked the door, smiled at me. I saw that she was drenched in sweat. Without saying anything, she again went towards the kitchen. I also didn't say anything. When I entered the living room, I was pleasantly surprised that everything was in its proper place, though there were not enough things. Radhika had already arranged and decorated whatever we had. I just went towards kitchen to see what she was up to, without even changing or freshening up. When I reached, I saw her preparing a meal for us. It was too hot to cook anything. She was oblivious of the fact that I was there, so without saying anything, I returned to the room, dragged the table fan and set the fan at the corner of the kitchen, just beside the door and switched it on. When it blew at her hair, she looked at the door, surprised. She moved her eyes downward, then towards me and smiled.

"What is my darling wife doing?" I came near her. To my surprise, she didn't react over this.

"Preparing a meal for us," she said. I didn't see what she was preparing. I just looked around.

"How was your day?" she asked.

"It's was good. Big office. Big salary. So big work," I said casually. "For that big salary, I came here. I like the work culture. People are supportive. Even my boss is good, quite intellectual. I wish I could have also studied as much as he did."

"That's good. Why don't you get freshened up? I will serve the meal," she said, taking out the plates.

"I will just be back and help you lay the table out. It's too hot in here for you to do everything," saying this, I left the kitchen.

After fifteen to twenty minutes, I went to the table, as she was setting up the plates. Looking at one plate, I asked, "Where is your plate?"

"I will eat once you finish eating," she said, turning towards the kitchen.

"No, we will eat together. No matter what," I said, followed her in so I could bring her plate.

We sat together on the table. When she put some vegetables on the plates, I was shocked to see its colour and texture, but didn't say anything. Looking at its colour, I prayed that at least the salt and other spices would be in the right amount. Then, something more shocking happened: when she took out two chapatis and kept on my plate, I saw that they were almost the shape of the world and black at places. I looked her, waiting her to speak first.

"I am sorry. I actually don't know how to make chapatis. At home, mummy ji used to make. This was the first time I did it by myself," she said. Her tone had a hint of an apology. Her face was twisted in nervousness. It seemed that she would break into tears at any moment.

I took a bite of the vegetable curry. Both were not edible on any count. Falsifying my prayers, the vegetable curry had excessive salt and less of other spices. But keeping my face normal, I said, "It's fine. Sometimes these things happen. Moreover, it's your first time. At least, I can see what vegetables are in this curry. When I cooked for the first time, you couldn't have even judged what vegetable it was." She smiled but it was a suppressed one. Because she too had realized by this time, as she had also managed to gulp down the curry. Anyhow, we finished the dinner. But I couldn't see any smile after we were done. I knew she was still brooding over this but I didn't mind it at all. I also knew that it wouldn't be effective to say anything at this moment. Her face had registered a disappointment. When I couldn't prevent myself from asking, I asked after a moment, while going towards the bedroom, "Is there something bothering you? And if it is about dinner, then I would say don't worry about that. I really liked it."

She didn't say anything, simply nodded. I noticed something from her eyes, a look of determination. I laughed at my own imagination hinting that she would be planning to join cooking classes now and not let me suffer with bad food at the end of a hard day at work.

I had left office with some pending work, and so was in living room, completing work on laptop. She had already gone to bed. When I crawled into the bed and made myself comfortable, I realized that she hadn't slept yet. Baffled, I whispered, "Radhika, are you awake?" Instead of answering, she took a deep breath in which made me feel that she was crying, still feeling sorry about the dinner.

"What's wrong?" I asked, and placed my hand over her shoulder in a hope that it could comfort her. After a moment, she turned around to face me. Her eyes were filled with tears. This was the second time when I saw tears in her eyes. The first time was when we were leaving for my home after the wedding. I looked into her eyes.

"I am sorry. I had cooked such bad food for you. You come home, so tired and I served such food for you," she whispered.

"Oh, dear. It happens. And honestly speaking, I enjoyed the food," I said, caressing her over her shoulder. "And I know you will learn it all very soon." I wiped her tears, pulled her cheeks. "You need not apologize."

"But it was very bad food. I know you are saying such words to comfort me. I also tasted those things, you know. Yukk! The curry was made of salt with vegetables for their flavour, it seemed.

The chapattis were burnt, twisted. I am such a bad wife," she sobbed.

I felt like laughing at her last line. "Who said you are a bad wife? You are so lovely. Don't worry. It is alright." After several reassurances, she felt a bit convinced and stopped sobbing.

Next morning, when I was coming out of the bathroom, I noticed surreptitiously that she was in the kitchen doing something. I slithered towards the kitchen, stood behind her, a few feet away and was completely surprised seeing her.

She was taking a spoonful of the tea from the pan. When it didn't satisfy her, she added some more sugar. Again, she took a spoonful to check whether it had proper sweetness or not. After three attempts, when it satisfied her, she poured it into the mugs and turned back with the tray in her hand. She turned so suddenly that I didn't have time to move away or hide. I was in a towel and vest.

"What are you doing here?" she asked.

"Nothing. Just seeing how my wife is taking care of everything."

Avoiding that, she replied, "And where are your clothes? If you get ready, I will serve you breakfast. Or you would be late for office."

Within a few days, she learnt to cook well. She spent lots of time in reading cook books, talking to her mummy or my mummy to learn some cooking skills. I was surprised at her speed and appreciated her effort. Next time, when she served me, I couldn't leave my dining table for at least thirty minutes. The food was delicious. I smiled at her, and she did too, and my heart filled with love for her.

It was the first instance of love being mentioned by bhaiya. 'Why does Naina's face keep coming into my thoughts?' I asked myself when after much attempt, I couldn't ignore her presence in my heart. I closed my eyes for a while and opened them again. Everything was silent, silent enough that I could easily hear the buzzing of crickets. I turned my head to the other side and dragged the curtain aside and took a peek at the sky. A plethora of stars were twinkling and the moonlight fell softly on the bed. I felt good but soon started thinking about the same thing. Instead of finding the answer for the same, my mind began throwing more images at me.

"Wake up, Akshat! We'll be late for college otherwise," she said and moved towards my table to arrange the books.

Lying on the costliest and softest mattress, I kept snoring soundly. I didn't hear her. In fact, I pulled the blanket over my head.

While arranging the table, her eyes stopped on a piece of paper and she held it up and turned around. "You got the result? You never told me."

She came near my bed, cast her glance over me and began shaking me, trying to wake me up. Since I was covered from head to toe, I groaned.

"Get up!" she cried out. "Wow, you have scored brilliantly." But she didn't get any response from me, and she pulled the blanket away in a fast stroke.

"Oh, god. What is this?" she screamed as if she saw a corpse beside my body.

"What? Why are you screaming? Can't you see that I am sleeping?" I sat, yawned, stretched my hands upward and said. But for a moment, she didn't turn back.

"What? What happened?" I asked curiously. Without saying any word, she indicated towards me with her one hand and other on her eyes, and it seemed she was trying hard to keep her eyes shut.

For a moment, I didn't understand but when she kept indicating towards me, I looked at myself. I was in underwear only. Seeing this, I screamed, "Holy cow! You saw everything?" and pulled the blanket again. I looked at her. She was shaking her head in a no, her eyes still covered, confirming that she hadn't seen anything. It was an accident.

I looked at her, frowning.

"Did I ask you to pull the blanket?" I asked.

"No, but I didn't know you sleep like this. Don't you dare to blame me for this. I was just waking you up," she said, "I have no interest seeing you and your disgusting things." She left the room in a huff.

"What? What!" I shouted, analyzing her last words but before that, she had gone out. I was so startled at her words that I ran after her, heading towards the door, in underwear. But as I realized that, I hid behind the door and I slammed my head against the door. The pain shot from the head down through the body. As I screamed, I saw Naina turning back but stopped when I shouted, "Don't even dare to turn around." I groaned and closed the door. Before that she threw a word of caution, "Press your head where you've hit it or a bump will surface." I didn't close the door.

"Hey, I am going to take a shower. You can come in the room and wait for me," I said.

11

Desperation, Desire and Dehradun

It had been several months since our marriage. I found myself looking at her every time she did something. Whether it was the kitchen or bedroom, I looked at her, at her face and the hair that fell on her face which she sometimes, annoyingly picked up and put behind her ear.

She was, of course, beautiful. Her skin was quite delicate to touch, and milky white. She had a naturally attractive face, perfectly chiselled, with big, hazel eyes, dark enough to hypnotize anyone. She had a good figure and maintained it. Seeing her coming out from her bath daily, in her towel, hair falling like a snake on her back, I found myself filled with longing to make love to her.

Yes, we hadn't made love to each other for all these months. I waited. It wasn't that I was desperate for it. We always had cheerful days together, but the closeness one could have shared in such a long period of time, we didn't have. What I craved was the desire in her eyes for me or a simple touch or gesture that would let me know she wanted me just as much as I longed for her. She affectionately talked to me all the time, but never hinted for such things. Sometimes, while watching movies or TV shows, when lovemaking scenes appeared on the screen, my eyes lingered over her face to see her expression or to observe what was going in her mind, but I couldn't understand anything. Something, anything that would signal we could take the next step. But how, I wondered, was I supposed to make this happen? It was for sure that she never complained about anything. I too had given her everything she wished for or was about to wish for, but I never found the great serenity or cheerfulness on her face that I wanted to see. Sometimes, it made me wonder if she felt she had made a mistake marrying me. I realized that this was not as easy as I'd originally thought it would be. There was something I was missing for sure. I had always led a simple life, but now, when I had started feeling for her, I didn't want to lose having those memorable moments. When this thought came across my mind, I decided to take the advice from my friends.

With the passage of time, I noticed that she eagerly waited for me, sitting in the drawing room, flipping through the pages of magazines or newspapers or sometimes watching TV. I would have never understood her anticipation as she had waited for me, until one day I observed it. That day, due to heavy work in office, I came one hour late. Due to heavy work, I had put my mobile on silent so that nothing could distract me. As I finished work, I rushed towards home, whispering, "Radhika will be waiting for me." I was in such a hurry to be home with her that I didn't even check my mobile phone.

When I reached, I thought Radhika would be angry at me but to my surprise, she didn't say anything and left the room, taking my bag. I sat in the hall, loosened my tie. She came with a glass of water, and politely asked, "How was your day? You are a little late in coming home today. Too much traffic?"

I stared at her. Her tone didn't have any hint of anger. It was calm, soothing and normal. I drank the glass of water, before replying, "No, it wasn't traffic. I got busy at work, lots of work."

"Oh, you are looking stressed. You take rest and freshen up. I prepared a nice, hot meal for you. Only chapatis are left to be made. I thought as you will come, I will serve it hot," she said. "By the way, I called you too."

"You called me? I didn't check," I said. "When?'

She had left the room but I heard her faint voice, echoing from the distance, "Forty times".

I hurriedly checked my mobile. It proudly showed forty missed calls.

Delhi summer was at its peak. I had noticed that for the past few weeks Radhika was not able to cope with the heat. All the time, she kept fanning herself with the handheld fan. Her forehead was covered with sweat almost all the time. The fans around the house were not enough. One night, when I didn't find her on the right side of the bed, I looked for her. It was early morning; I checked my mobile phone and saw that it was 4 a.m. I got off the bed, looked into the other rooms. I directed myself to balcony as the balcony gate lay open. She was there, standing in the light breeze. The surroundings were silent, and since I was barefoot, she didn't get any hint that I was there.

"Radhika, you are here!" I heaved a sigh of relief. She turned suddenly.

"Yes, it was too humid inside and I was not able to sleep. So came out," she said.

I understood. For the past few days, I had noticed this. Radhika never said anything but I understood.

On the same evening, I returned home from office at the usual time. Radhika opened the door, with a beaming face.

"Hi, did anyone come today?" I asked.

"No! No one," she replied. "I will bring you a glass of water." As she was about to leave the room, there was a knock on the door. We looked at each other. We both went towards to see who that was.

"Mr. Randhir?" a man of average height dressed in formal attire asked in a polite tone.

"Yes."

"Sir, I have come from Gupta Electronics. You had ordered for an air conditioner," he said. "Sorry sir, we are a bit late."

Listening to this, Radhika looked at me and whispered, "What is this?" I smiled at her and replied in whisper, "Solution for this summer." She remained puzzled over my action.

"Yes, yes. I was waiting for you. Please fit the air conditioner." After few minutes, a short man with dishevelled hair came in with a carton that contained the packed air conditioner and within an hour, they fitted the air condition in our bedroom and left.

As he left the room, Radhika spoke suddenly as if she had been waiting for them to leave, "Why did you buy the air conditioner? It's so costly."

"Costly? What is the use of money if we can't satisfy our needs?" I said.

"Still..." she couldn't complete her sentence before I interrupted her again.

"Radhika, I have seen you, covered in sweat all night. Waiting for dawn so that you could have some cool air again and passing the night in restlessness. This can ruin your health," I said, looking directly into her eyes.

She didn't say anything and moved towards the kitchen for a cup of tea. After that she had easy nights of sleep.

Days had been passing but the attention I was seeking, I didn't get. But looking at initial plan to get her attention, I didn't stop trying.

In July, after seven months of marriage, I decided to surprise her on a Friday evening. In between, I read numerous books on relationships, some suggested by my colleague and some I found in the magazine stands.

On that evening, when I came back in the evening, at the same usual time, she was watching TV. I greeted her with a smile and asked," How was your day today? I remember you have doctor's appointment?" and handed over her my office bag.

"Bit bored in the noon. Yes, doctor has nothing to say. It's all fine," she responded gracefully, "You might be starving. I will make tea for you."

"Why only for me? Tea for us?" I said and smiled. She reciprocated the same. As she left the room, I quickly took out the piece of paper where I had written that recipe and revised all the ingredients with quantity. I bought a cookbook and planned to prepare dinner on Friday. She arrived with tray carrying two cups of tea; I was freshened up and was sitting on the couch.

After that, I didn't know why I couldn't say anything to her.

As usual, I returned from the office at the same time, kept the office bag at the same place. Earlier, I just used to throw it on the sofa. But I saw that Radhika, without saying a word, picked up my bag and kept it at the right place. It embarrassed me and I learned from it. It is the best quality in Radhika that she never says anything hurtful. So, after changing clothes, I sat down and was relaxing in the room. I was seated on my comfortable couch stretching my legs, watching TV but she came into room holding a tray with cups and a pot, I arranged myself in a proper way.

"Evening tea!"

"Waah!" I exclaimed and stretched my hand to take my plate. I was happy to see the tea. Work really tired me. There was another thing to be happy. But I thought I'd tell Radhika in another wonderful way. She again left the room.

On seeing her, I asked, holding my plate in hand, "Where are you going? Please sit."

She didn't turn back but before going completely out of the room, she said, "Coming in a minute."

I didn't give another thought over this and started sipping my tea watching TV. After a minute or two, she came back to the room with her hands carrying a plate of hot *pakodas*.

First I thought that our unfamiliarity made things so complex and made a barrier between us, that we needed to remove these obstacles. I even noticed that our dinner conversations, for instance, were bound to a certain topic though we always ate our dinner together. After forty minutes, when she again left the room to make dinner, I thought I'd ask her. But then decided not to, for it would be quite odd for her. So, I thought of another way.

I went into the kitchen behind her, took an apple from the dining table and said in a very normal tone, "Radhika, you know, quite often, when Mom-Dad left me to visit some relative's house, for a wedding or some other occasion, I tried my hand at cooking too."

I was surprised that while giving my excuse, how easily words flowed out and even seemed so natural.

"Oh, okay," she said and kept cutting the vegetables.

When it didn't interest her, I tried to take forward the conversation, "I remember, at first I was quite angry at my parents about how can they leave me alone. I didn't know how to cook and I got bored eating outside at food stalls. So, one night, I decided to cook by myself." Though her eyes were not on me, it seemed that she was listening to me now. When I saw that she was almost done with of the preparation for cooking and was getting ready to put the utensils on the stove, I accelerated my idea to convince her.

"It wasn't all of a sudden. Actually, I was inspired from some cooking show at that time. Even, you know, I shifted my TV to the kitchen so that I could follow the recipe."

Listening this, she laughed. I felt relieved. "So, what I was thinking was… that I could cook the same dish today for us. I never did know at that time if I cooked well. Let's see if I did?" Listening to this, she stopped working. I too had finished eating the apple. "But I have cut all the vegetables."

"Aah, don't worry about that. Most surprisingly, I need these vegetables only. Though the size is bit different, but who knows, it may taste better now that you have touched them." She smiled, and I am sure I blushed. O cover up, I quickly added, "You just sit on the couch in the living room and watch TV."

She smiled and asked, "Are you sure?"

"Hundred and ten percent. You just wait and watch. I will call you when I will set the table with a surprise."

"Surprise? What?" she asked, standing at the kitchen door.

"Surprise is a surprise. I will tell you at that time." And she left the kitchen.

'Well, Mister. Let's see how your mind manipulates all these things?' I realised I was talking to myself. First I cursed and then questioned to myself, which brought a smile on my face.

Looking at the way in which the vegetables had been cut, I decided to make them as a starter because I already had another menu for the main course. I tried to remember the recipe, but when I couldn't remember all the ingredients, I sneaked around and walked slowly towards my office bag and took out the recipe. In half an hour, salad and mixed dried vegetables starters was ready. Looking at it, I felt a sense of relief. Deep within, I was exalted.

For the main course, I thought of making a paneer gravy curry and pulao to serve it with. I had cottage cheese, cumin seeds, curry leaves, onions, chopped tomato, and other spices that were required. Soon, the smell of spices filled the kitchen. On the other stove, I kept the cooker for the rice.

It was ten more minutes to finish and serve the plates, when Radhika called me out, "Are you done with cooking? What you are cooking for so long?" her tone was calm, not agitated. As against mine; I used to show my agitation when she, sometimes, took time for cooking. And in turn, I always felt sorry when I saw that on the table she had served for me something special.

"No, not yet. Ten more minutes. What are you doing?" I asked, taking out the pulao and serving it on the plates.

"I took a bath and now am watching TV," she said.

When I served and finished setting all the plates properly, I thought about calling her. Then out of impulse, I lit two candles and kept them in the centre of the table.

"I am done. Now, you can come in, Radhika," I called out to her.

When she rounded the corner, I was struck by how radiant she looked. Her silky and shining hair clearly indicated that she had just washed it. She had tucked a few strands behind her ear, and she was wearing a salwar suit with a pendant hanging around her neck.

She looked at me, smiled and then shifted her look towards the dining table and widening her eyes she said, "Wow!" At the same time, I also said looking at her marvellous beauty and said, "Wow!"

When it happened, we started laughing and I asked, "Wow for what?"

"No, first you tell me. Your wow was for what?"

"Umm... Wow... Umm," I didn't know how to begin as I had never done it before. So, I took a moment. She kept looking at my face. I saw a beauty, a charm on her face that I had never seen before. It seemed that what Neeta, my colleague, had said in office had come true. She tried to read my face but my confused face couldn't bring any reply to her question.

"For what?" she prodded.

"You are looking very beautiful," I said in one sentence.

She smiled but averted her eyes from me and started looking downward. I smiled at her too. "Okay then! I have done everything. Dinner is ready. Shall we start?" Listening to this, she raised her eyebrows, nodded and walked towards the table.

I took the chair and asked that she sit opposite me, so that I could see her all the time. It always felt great to see her while having dinner. Moreover, that day was special. I started uncovering the dishes and served her.

"Oh my god, you cooked all this," she took a bite of the appetizer. Her radiant face was showing that she liked the food. "It's delicious. Really! I didn't know that you cook so well." She opened another pot containing the paneer dish and took a bite of it, her favourite dish, chewed it slowly, enjoying every bit of it.

I smiled and felt myself exhale in relief. After sometime, she asked, "You were saying that there is one more surprise. Where is that?"

"Oh! I forgot. One minute," I said, hiding my pleasure and pulled an envelope from the shirt pocket and gave it to her.

"What is this?"

"Surprise!" I said happily.

She took it and opened it.

I studied her face, I noticed that the way she used to confine was now bit relieved but when she started reading that page, her face took the expression of excitement that I hadn't ever seen till date, and I could tell what she was feeling. I had been holding my breath.

She read it enthusiastically as I anticipated looking at her moving eyes and with time, she gained the spark of elation. She looked at me and said keeping her tone cheerful, "This is an appointment letter. You got a job that you wanted."

"Yes, and if you would come to know the package they are offering, you will be happier!" I said trying to make her more cheerful.

"Yes, I am waiting to know it,"

"Ten lakh annually, plus benefits that include free trips and others perks. Now, we can easily pay the home loan off and live a better life."

"Oh, wow. Now I know why you made this occasion so special."

"Yes, but the credit goes to you. Everything is changing around me after you have come into my life," I said. She felt good as her face gleamed, and her cheeks went from pink to red, but to change the topic, she asked popping into her mouth another bit of food, "These are really good. How did you learn these recipes?" she had an enthusiastic tone.

"No, not really. I just followed the recipe," I said smirking and pulled out the piece of paper of recipe.

"Oh!" and she started laughing with obvious joy at my innocence as I hadn't tried to act smart.

Everything seemed so beautiful at that moment and the easy mood between us lasted till we finished eating dinner and she started cleaning the table. I too helped her. In between, our banter kept the moment light. And as she laughed and chatted, I felt as if my heart had just been filled with the joy of such moments. Perhaps it was the first time after our wedding reception that we shared such moments together and the flame of closeness started burning within me. When we reached the sink with the plates, she said keeping plates in the sink, "Today, Maa called me."

"Oh, how is she?" I asked.

"She is fine."

I stood just behind her, close enough to easily catch her sweet smell, which rushed my heartbeat. Almost there, I realized, but when I was close enough to touch her hand, she didn't react. It seemed that it was sudden touch. She kept speaking but for me, I was just pulling myself towards her. On no reply, she turned back, but felt startled as our faces were really close. Her eyes widened, our face moved towards each other and she closed her eyes, knowing at the moment what was going on and soon, our lips touched. It was the first kiss and I would remember it forever.

I didn't push it beyond our initial comfort. After this evening, as I reached home after office every day, I continued to watch her, pretending to be working. Sometimes, we went to sleep together; some other times, she left early after clearing the dining table, washing the sink and spending few moments with me before saying, "Okay, I am going to sleep. Are you going to work or sleep?"

"Yeah, you would be tired. You better go and take rest," I said raising my eyes from the laptop. "I have some work to finish.

You know these private companies. They buy you with their money." And I chuckled.

She always left saying goodnight to me and I too reciprocated the same, with the same sincerity in my voice. I remember in such situations, I never worked for more than half an hour or forty five minutes after she had left for the bedroom.

One day, the same thing happened and I went to the room after finishing my work. When I slid into bed, I inferred from her movements that she was awake.

"Radhika, are you awake?" I asked.

"Mmm," she answered automatically. From her tone, I presumed that she was trying to sleep, but hadn't been successful.

"I am thinking something."

"About what?" she continued in the same tone without looking at me, since she had her back towards me.

"As I haven't taken any leave from the office for quite a long time, why don't I apply for a leave for two weeks and we shall go somewhere."

My words finally registered and she sat up.

"Where?" she asked.

"Anywhere? Wherever you wish. There are several holiday spots. After marriage, we didn't go for our honeymoon."

That word made her blush a little, me too. "But what is the need to take a holiday? You have just joined the office," she hesitated.

"Oh, don't worry about that. Even my boss was saying that I could take holiday break as I have been continuously working since I have joined the office." I said, "If I don't take those leaves, the off-days I have will lapse."

"But where would we go? I have no idea."

"Just away from this noisy place. Any place where we could spend time together without any disturbance. Moreover, you also work so hard. From the crack of dawn till night," I said. I noticed that she also sat up against the wall and leaned her head on my shoulder. It felt great to find her coming so close to me. I also wrapped my hand around her waist.

"Okay, then I will check on the internet about some such place and will also apply for leave," I said. At that, she said yes and I felt her head nodding against my shoulder.

On the scheduled day, we left Delhi for Dehradun. We arrived in the evening but the sun was still in the sky. I had already booked the best suite in the hotel. The person on the reception welcomed us when I told him about our reservation on asking. The bell boy carried our luggage, which was only two trolley bags.

"Sir, this is your room. Please feel comfortable," he said in an amicable tone and entered the room. Radhika and I looked around.

"From here, you can enjoy the sunset and the lush green, the seductive beauty of nature," he again said, opening the door of the balcony.

"Happy stay and make your trip enjoyable and memorable. Please let us know if you need anything. For now, shall we send some tea or coffee?" He asked.

"Yeah, tea and coffee both, please," I said.

"Sure sir. Please give us a few minutes. Thanks," he said, smiling a great deal and left the room.

Before dinner, sensing some nervousness in Radhika, I asked her if we could go for walk. As I found the environment so soothing to my nerves, I thought it would be romantic to take a walk together. The air held neither the humidity of summer, nor the chill of winter. It was pleasant, fresh to the face.

She agreed and we moved out of the resort. With a small hand bag in hand, we walked past the residential areas and strolled towards the road, lit up by the yellow street lights but there was still the sun at the tip of the horizon on the other end, almost on the verge of drowning. Its redness still prevented darkness to spread over the sky. I carefully checked around to see where we could go and then took the first path we saw, because it did not matter.

For the first few minutes, none of us spoke anything but as we strolled for some distance, I wanted to speak first. Walking closely to her, I didn't say anything because when I looked towards her, I was mesmerized seeing her.

Radhika kept her gaze fixed straight ahead, her back straight and her pace steady. Her cherry coloured heels clicked against the ground and her hair waved with the breeze. November had begun and there was a slight nip in the air. She wore a black jacket, not exactly an overcoat, but larger than usual. A cream coloured bag was hanging over her shoulder and her hair, shoulder length and impeccably trimmed, was blowing softly. I liked everything about her, whenever she touched my hand, I felt pleased and didn't make any attempt to remove my hand. I remembered that I was about to say something.

"It's so beautiful," I said looking around at the thousand shades of green graced trees.

She nodded and whispered, "It's really beautiful and very peaceful." I looked at her and smiled.

Really, it was a very beautiful place. Silent roads with random flowers at their sides; the air filled with the sweet chirrup of birds that hid in the leaves of trees. It was like music in the air.

After a few moments of silence, and some words, she also seemed to be enjoying my company, and this brought a smile on my face. My purpose to come here, it seemed, had started fulfilling.

It feels ridiculous when a husband or wife finds it difficult or shy to hold each other's hands. But, it felt great when our hands kept touching. As it got touched, she used to avert her hand slightly. I too didn't make any attempt to reach her hand forcefully, but after a few brief touches, our fingers intertwined. It was so full of love that I felt myself get carried away and so did she. When she squeezed my hand, first, I looked at her, but she was looking straight, then I glanced away, felt something new to my senses. We didn't uncurl our fingers.

I paused after a certain distance and moved in front of her. She suddenly stopped and her eyebrows moved up in surprise.

"What is it?" she asked. "Don't you want to go further?"

"I want to go further. But for a few days, something is stirring within me."

"And what is that?"

"Are you happy with me Radhika? It seems that sometimes marriage with me has brought a disappointment for you. Is it so?"

Her eyes widened with surprise. "What made you say that?"

"I was just curious. I didn't know what to do in a relationship. We had an arranged marriage."

I waited for her response, I wondered if she guessed the reason behind my question. She stared at me for a moment, as if trying to read my mind.

"Yes, we had an arranged marriage. Well, initially things were a bit dull but now it's good," she said, drawing a long breath.

"Really? You know that's why I decided to plan a vacation. It gives time to understand each other." I smiled saying this. She too joined me.

"Ok, tell me one thing. Had you ever been in any relationship earlier?" she asked.

"No, never. I am usually a reserved type of person, right from childhood. It is true that I was quite studious. And you know, girls come close to studious boys only for notes," I smirked saying this.

She too started laughing. "It's not like that."

"Maybe. But that was what I experienced."

"Oh, and how did the idea of cooking for me came to you that night?" she asked in a curious tone.

"Oh," I tried to think of a reason but when I couldn't find any suitable reasons, I decided to be honest with her, "To be honest, I thought I was not able to keep you happy. So to bring some vitality in our relationship, I asked some advice from an office colleague. She was with me during my college days. And also knows that I can cook. So, she advised me to cook for you. I took the recipe from some cook book."

"But I didn't see you reading any cook book," she said.

"Actually, I read that in office and left it there," I smiled sheepishly.

"Really?"

"It is true." I made an apologetic face, and she nodded, her face suffused with a glow that also brought happiness and satisfaction to me. After that we didn't talk much, enjoying the silence, feeling the love, the unspoken love. She too said nothing, nor asked anything. She had tugged the collar of her cardigan closed as if preparing for a wave of bitter cold to come, looking straight ahead with her lips drawn into a perfectly straight line. When I saw her shaking, I covered her with my own coat.

Though when we came out for stroll, the sky was cloudless or it had some flecks of clouds scattered over the blue sky, but within an hour, the weather started to change. The wind started blowing – cold, damp and gentle. And the clouds rolled directly overhead, covering the sun, leaving the surroundings with little light. Everything soon turned so romantic, and I saw that Radhika was also enjoying this change in weather. I didn't say anything to her as she opened her arms for the breeze, but carefully watched her. Looking her this way, I thought I had made the right decision in coming here. Soon the wind became stronger, gushing towards us from every direction and accompanied by the rain, a light sprinkle like someone was spraying water from the clouds. I looked around. The few people and couples who were strolling had increased their pace to reach their destination soon, and I saw that road was empty. The light already had become dim. I thought I should ask Radhika that to go to the hotel but as I was about to say this, she said, "Wow. It's raining. It's my favourite weather. I love rain and love dancing in it."

I could not say anything, when I saw that she took some more steps, walked ahead of me and started dancing without being afraid of getting wet. Seeing this, I dropped my idea and stood where I had been. It was really soothing to see her like this, enjoying herself. I saw that she opened herself up and she ran her hands through her hair. The clothes were getting wet but she didn't care about it. I smiled at her childishness. With time, the drops were becoming thicker, the sky darkened more and rain started falling hard. It felt wonderful. It was the first time that I had deliberately stopped and allowed myself to get wet in the rain. But it was amazing. I was unaware of such beauty till date.

I saw that Radhika, forgetting everything, was enjoying the rain. She raised her head towards the sky to let the raindrops hit her face. She knew that her clothes were soaked in the rain but she didn't care.

I was smiling. She stopped dancing when she saw that I was standing still. She called me but her words were suppressed beneath the falling of the rain and the wind that carried her words away from me. She called me gesturing her hands but I signalled a no. When I didn't come, she walked towards me and held my hand, dragged me onwards the centre of the road and started dancing. Her mood was so exuberant that I did nothing except observe her. Her steps. Her hair hanging in front was moving here and there. I tried to read into the pleasure in her eyes. When she tried to make me dance a few times, I tried too. Looking at my clumsy dancing, she started laughing. I joined her. Then suddenly, a cloud burst directly above us and the rain began to come down even harder. She came closer to me and embraced me. Even through the rain, I could hear her deep, fast breathing.

I didn't know how she was feeling, but for me it was a different hug. Something deep, tight and passionate. I embraced her in the same way, with no track of time. She was completely nestled in my chest and my hands were coiled her around her waist. I felt the warmth with my fingers moving slowly across her back. Just feeling her so close to me made me feel something different that day. I assumed she was feeling the same as she didn't make any attempt to stop my hand from slithering across her body. Her clothes were soaked in rain, and I could easily observe and feel the outline of her beautiful body, and I had to take several deep breaths to calm this feeling. But I knew it was useless. Her chest squeezed against mine. Her silence over this made me realize that lots of things had changed between us.

When the rain became softer, we walked holding hands and we understood, as we looked at each other, and her lips full of subtle charm confirmed the mutual realization that we had fallen in love with each other. It was better than ever. While coming back to hotel, we crossed the lover's points, whereupon seeing young couples sitting behind bushes or sitting on the benches, kissing each other, made our feelings stronger. First we avoided seeing this, later after crossing the lover's point, we broke into a laugh and for the rest of way, she rested her head on my arm. There was no uneasiness between us by the time we reached the hotel.

"Sir, would you like to have your dinner in our dining room or in your suite?" the waiter asked.

"In the room, but we will call you," Radhika said.

"Thank you." and he left.

As we entered the room, I said, "You change your clothes; I will also change mine. We shouldn't fall sick."

She nodded her head, still feeling the roll of emotions within her. I smiled at her, which was duly reciprocated.

I changed into a pyjama and t-shirt; she was in her night wear, a sleeveless one.

"Did you take a bath?" I asked.

"No," she replied, without turning back as she was looking into the mirror. "It felt great, the feeling of rain on the skin." She dried her hair, and brushed it but didn't pin it, let it fall on the shoulder.

When she was doing this, I walked up to the fireplace, poked the fire and put some wooden logs. The temperature outside had fallen and brought some chill in the surrounding. She too joined me on the sofa opposite to me and rested her hand on the armrest. In a few minutes, the fire had turned into flames.

"Shall we order our dinner?" I asked.

"Yes," And I ordered the food. The room boy served the dinner and left the room. She started plating the food and I kept catching a glimpse of her out of the corner of my eyes.

"I think you are not comfortable. Shall I bring you a quilt?" I asked when I saw her adjusting her clothes quite a few times.

"Yes," and I brought her a quilt. The flame in the fireplace was quite steady. I put in some more logs and began our dinner.

Thunder boomed loudly outside and we could hear the rain pattering outside. But the flickering heat of the logs provided some relief from the chill. She stood and turned towards the window.

"The weather is lovely. Isn't it?" she asked and returned to the sofa.

"Yeah, and I think it is going to be this way the whole night," I said.

"Yeah, I like this. This sound of rain. It's some kind of nature's music. Feels so relieving and smooth to the heart and mind." She said, chewing a piece of naan. "I have liked this season since I have been a girl. Once I caught cold and had high fever, then my father stopped me from dancing in the rain. But I never listened to him," she smiled, reviving old memories.

"Anything special related to this weather?" I asked.

"No, nothing particular. I find it too romantic."

"I love this weather too," I said. I had never had much inclination towards such weather but after what had happened today, it was quite special to me. Soon, we finished our dinner.

I saw that her eyelids were dropping now, so I asked, "You are feeling sleepy?"

"Yes, but it's fine," she said without turning back.

"Anyhow, it's night," I said.

Later, when I did at last crawl into bed, she already was there. I slipped under the blanket and tuned my face towards her face. She was breathing steadily and I could see her serene face. I stared at her, so peaceful, so charming. Without disturbing her, it seemed that I just wanted to keep staring at her face without waking her up. It was so lovely. A few strands of hair had fallen on her face. I adjusted myself to see her without any obstacles in between, and my hand touched with her. He skin was so soft, and so delicate. It felt magical touching her.

Suddenly, she opened her eyes, and asked, "What are you staring at?"

I felt embarrassed at this and mumbled, "Nothing, just staring at my beautiful wife."

I felt her hand over me, wrapping itself around my chest. She just stuck herself to me, and put her head on my shoulder. It was relieving. Looking into those sparkling eyes which overflow with nothing but unspoken love for each other was such a delight.

"You know, I had never been much into the emotional bit of life. I have always struggled to make life better for my family. But whatever is happening in its aftermath is so wonderful, so lovely. When I look at you, I see something beautiful in you, in our relationship and our future. I have spent my life just fulfilling the basic needs of life and never paid any attention towards this. But now, it seems so fine," I said, holding her hand. I realized that she had started squeezing my hands, looking at me without blinking. I also looked back at her with all the love that I could gather. She was looking so beautiful and lovely that I couldn't measure anything at that time and leaned against her, felt the warmth of her body. It was the perfect moment of togetherness that we had earned with time. That night, we made love for the first time.

"Now, everything feels right about life," she looked at me with her deep, hazel eyes and I kissed her softly. She brought her hand to my face, touched me, brushing it softly against my skin. I kissed her everywhere, on her neck, her eyes, her nose, her lips, and forehead. Her skin was so smooth. These months of separation had turned our union into a very sweet moment.

As she opened her eyes, a sense of satisfaction was radiating from her eyes. I smiled seeing this. We came near the fireplace again but she sat on my lap. Holding her hands, like the fire curling around the wood logs, kissing on her neck, I said: "You know from now, we will never leave each other. No matter what happens, we will eat in the same plate. I will call you every day from office. And I will never go out alone. I'd want you to be with me all the time. Because I love you."

She smiled, and her eyes lit up as she held my face and murmured, "I love you too."

Next evening under the shawl of dusk, we set out for another walk, taking another path to explore new places around us. Fiddling with her hands in mine, I sometimes, after taking a quick peek around to ensure nobody was looking, put light kisses on her neck. The road was lush with green trees on the both sides and was so long, that one would have to tilt his neck to see its complete length. We had walked for almost half-an-hour, when Radhika motioned me to stop. She waved her hand towards a house on the opposite side of the road. "That's beautiful. Isn't it?"

It was a small wooden house, with a patio. The fence was also wooden, and it had a small door. Around the fences, the bushes had grown wildly in irregular shapes. The roof of that wooden house was triangular, with slopes on both sides so that rain water could tumble down properly. Then my eyes stuck over a board. A white wooden board over which was written something in big, black letters. We could not see what it said from the distance. We crossed the road, went near the house. On the board was written FOR SALE.

"That's beautiful. I mean, it's a quaint and small cottage," she said, looking at the cottage, and we walked a few more steps towards that small gate.

"Yes," my eyes were wide with interest. I followed her, went inside that house along with Radhika.

We inspected the home. Radhika was very happy seeing this cottage and I thought it'd be a fine idea if we could own this place. We could visit the city where our love found a new meaning and relive those moments. Having a cottage here would only help with the accommodation problem. It was an investment for the future, our future. Not much later, I bought it. You are sitting inside it right now and it looks all well-maintained, but at that time, this cottage's wall had a dull and sickly look. It had to be painted and repaired, but it was worth the effort. You can see it now, it smells of love, it is resplendent with love.

12

Reminiscences

For a few months after this honeymoon, it was impossible to say whether it was Dehradun or love that had changed us so radically. We came back with a new conception of life that took our lives on a roller coaster ride and everything went perfectly well.

We tried our best to build a relationship filled with love, care and trust. We always enjoyed dinner together, no matter how late I got at office. She would wait for me, without touching her food. Sometimes she surprised me by serving my favourite dishes, which really filled my heart with enormous love for her. I used to be so surprised when she didn't even counter my explanations for being late. I understood this and tried to do something to keep her cheerful. Whenever I saw her smiling face, all my fatigue left me. There were times when I picked up roses on my way back from work to surprise her, sometimes took her out for her favourite cuisine, or with new clothes.

One evening, I remembered that it was Sunday evening when we went to the mall for shopping. We had been lucky to have some relief from the scorching summer heat, and the sky was covered with clouds without any sign of rain. So we decided to go out to buy some household items.

After our shopping list was all ticked out, I asked Radhika, "Shall we have pizza?" She nodded. Then we headed towards Pizza Hut. As we were heading towards the shop, my eyes got stuck on the mannequin in the shop that was two shops before Pizza Hut. My foot paused for a moment. The mannequin was in a night dress, a skimpy one, low cut and transparent. Its length was so short that it hardly reached the knee. Looking at the mannequin, a naughty thought crawled into my mind. When I averted my eyes after a brief appraising to Radhika, to my surprise, she was looking at me. I felt embarrassed, as the mischievous smile was still there on my face, and I forcefully tried to make a normal face. On the way to Pizza Hut, we didn't say anything.

I was thinking about a way to buy that night gown while we ordered pizza and waited for it. I was confused as I couldn't buy it in front of her, for I was sure she won't let me buy it. I had to find some way to leave her for a few minutes so that I could go and buy it, but I had to do it surreptitiously. None of us spoke anything till the pizza came.

Taking a slice of pizza in her mouth, Radhika said, "Is there anything else to buy?"

When she asked this, I stopped for a moment holding my half eaten pizza as it seemed that she understood my naughty idea but to falsify this, I said, stammering, "No. I don't think so." She nodded. Then I suddenly spoke, realizing my plan, "I have to buy a tie for an upcoming meeting. I have to give a presentation."

"Okay, I have to buy some cosmetics too," Radhika said.

"Oh, fine. I will buy the tie in the other shop. You can buy your cosmetics till then," I said, smiling to myself, as she didn't know what was going on in my mind. When she paused and looked at me, trying to figure out what was going on, I asked, "Do you have money with you?"

"I have money. Five hundred," she said.

"Only five hundred? I guess it won't be enough," I said, took my wallet out of my pocket, and pulled a few five hundred rupee notes out. "Keep this with you. You may need it."

We paid the bill for the pizza and came out. I looked around to check whether there was any tie shop nearby, and I found a *Van Heusen* showroom just three shops away.

"Here is the showroom. I will buy the tie there," I said. "From where would you buy the cosmetics?" I was deliberately getting her out of my way.

"Oh! It's downstairs. I will go there now. You can join me when you're done," she said. When she said this, I knew my way was clear.

She went downstairs and I quickly went to the tie shop and bought one hurriedly. After verifying that she had entered the shop, I walked slowly towards the lingerie shop. I felt uncomfortable going inside, especially without the lady by my side. I could see ladies undergarments hanging all around me. First I thought it was better to leave. As I moved towards the gate, a woman's voice spoke to me politely.

"Sir, may I help you?"

I turned back to face the saleswomen.

She again repeated, "How can I help you?"

"Hmm.. Umm. I want to buy a nightgown for my wife," I said, and the words came out so naturally.

"Sure, sir," she replied and showed me several nightgowns. I was feeling very uncomfortable as most of the nightgowns she showed me were so short that I wondered where the cloth was used exactly. Still that mannequin's nightgown was far better. When I liked nothing else, I requested them to show me that same gown the mannequin was wearing. They showed it, and I requested them to pack it.

I watched attentively as she was packing it in a big carton.

I interrupted her: "Excuse me! Can you pack this gown in some small packet?" First she wondered why, but respectfully obeyed my request.

I quickly hid the small packet in the shopping bags and came down to the shop where Radhika had gone. Radhika was paying her bills. She glanced at me and asked, "Don't you think that packet is too big for a tie?"

I didn't expect this question. I paused for a moment, looked at her steady face, and was thinking of coming up with a proper reason.

"What happened to you?' she asked, puzzled.

"Aah, no, nothing. You know, these brands pack even small things in big packets to make it look more attractive."

When she gave a satisfied chuckle, I felt relief. Eating ice creams, that I bought for her even after she refused several times, we came back home.

One morning, at the time of serving breakfast, even before she could join me on the table, her face took some distorted shape as she gestured to indicate that something was rising up from inside her stomach. She clutched her stomach, and then covered her mouth. She hurriedly walked, almost ran towards the washbasin. I didn't understand this, so I followed her with anxiety, leaving everything on the dining table as it was. She stopped in front of the washbasin, looked at the mirror, pressing against her mouth, but when it became unbearable, she buried her face in the washbasin, and with gurgling sounds, she retched out everything.

"Are you okay? Radhika?" I asked anxiously.

She didn't speak a thing, her face buried inside the basin even now. When nothing more came out, she raised her face, looked into the mirror. Her eyes were sore and red, and her face had lost its liveliness.

I was standing there, right behind her.

"Are you okay, Radhika?" I again asked. She wheezed.

Flushing out the basin, she turned towards me. I put my palms over her cheeks, trying to make her feel good.

Her face beamed. I was relieved when I saw that she was fine.

A week later, I was standing right behind her in the kitchen, caressing her hair. She turned back to me suddenly and said with a mesmerising smile, "I guess I am carrying our child and you are going to be a father soon."

"What!!"

She nodded to confirm it.

For a moment, I was stunned and then suddenly I started dancing like a mad man. My happiness was out of control. I lifted her up in my arms, came out of the kitchen to dining spaces and danced holding her. Her face lit up seeing me so happy. In between, she even tried to say something but I deliberately didn't listen, continued my hysterical happiness and dance. After fifteen minutes of my madness, I put her down.

A little hesitantly, she told me that her parents had called.

She said that papa and mummy will be leaving for Jammu.

"Jammu? How so suddenly?" I asked.

"Yes, they will be going to the Vaishno Devi temple," she said, folding a sari. She stopped, stepped ahead, and kept the sari in the almirah. I waited for her to say something as I had the hint that she wanted to ask or say something.

"What I was thinking was that..." she paused, then looked at me and added, "...I would like to go with them. It was my eternal wish that I visit that temple and pray at Mata's darbar. And it has been months since I have seen my parents. "

I hesitated over this. But looking at her face, I nodded. "When are your parents leaving for Jammu? I have to book tickets for you."

Listening to this, she wondered and looked puzzled. "Do you want me to go?"

"Yeah, why not! You want to go the temple. It's an auspicious occasion too. I am not sending you forever," I said.

"But who will take care of you?" she grew pensive.

"Aah, don't worry about that. I will manage," I tried to relax her. By now, she had folded all her clothes and kept them in their proper place.

On the scheduled date, which was five days later, Radhika left for her mother's home. I went to the railway station to send her off.

"Please take care of yourself. And come back soon," I said. "Call me regularly."

"*Haan baba.* Okay, listen. Take care of yourself too. I have asked Radha to cook for you," she replied. Radha was the maid at our home. Within a minute, the train signalled its departure. We exchanged our goodbyes. I kept watching the train till it vanished from my sight and then I returned home.

She called me after reaching. She was excited to go on the trip and also informed that they would leave for Jammu two days later. I too wanted to join them but the busy schedule of my job didn't allow me a single day off. I even applied for two days' leave but they rejected it.

The day Radhika reached Vaishno Devi, something peculiar happened to me that shook me.

It was an ordinary Sunday, no different from the other days except that it was a holiday, a relief from my busy schedule at work. I woke up at my usual time, at seven in the morning, but I was not in my bedroom but on the leather sofa. I didn't remember when I had fallen asleep at night. I got up from the sofa and stretched my body which had started aching now and sat down on sofa, yawned and stretched my legs. While rotating my body, my eyes fell on a photo album. That was our honeymoon album. She was leaning over my shoulder. I started missing her terribly. At that instant, I called her. Her phone was unreachable.

I kept my phone on the table and whispered, "It might be that there's no network." Then my eyes shifted and got focused on a sweater that my mother had sent me the previous day. I cheerfully picked up the sweater in my hand. It was beautiful and I liked it at first glance. I went back reminiscing how I never listened to my mother about my marriage. I always averted this talk whenever she tried to broach this topic with a usual answer: everything would be fine. I will marry and you will have lots of grand children. And she always responded to my answers delightfully. I kept the sweater back and moved towards the bathroom. After coming out, I made a cup of coffee for myself.

Sitting down, I lifted my gaze and looked outside of window, pulling the curtains aside and felt something good, pleasurable in my mind. It was a peaceful view of a remote part of the apartments. A few elderly people were jogging and chatting with their friends in gardens shadowed with trees; sunlight was falling gently on the children on the other side of the apartment complex, who were playing hide and seek. One boy, about two or three years old was crying uncontrollably, sitting on a park bench as he felt desolate when none included him in their game, which reminded me of my childhood. I smiled.

Without much thought, I dug out my camera from the almirah and started clicking their pictures. When I was done, I came back into the room. I didn't know anyone from this apartment, although it was ten storey apartment complex and a lot of people lived there. I didn't even know who my neighbour. Living alone gave me some independence; I grew the habit of eating at an early time and thankfully, the maid had cooked food early that day. Because I had missed my dinner last night, I was incredibly hungry. It was the fifth time that I was opening my refrigerator door to get something out of it to eat, but I took out the same coke and cake that I had eaten the last four times. The maid hadn't come yet, maybe because it was a holiday and she was taking it easy too. I started missing Radhika. In spite of feeling hungry, I was not angry and I patiently waited for the maid to come. To kill time, I picked a novel that I had bought a few days back and flipped through its pages. Reading book helped me pass some time, but after reading a few pages, I kept it aside and picked up the remote and turned on the TV.

I didn't register how much time I had spent like that, and remained engrossed in the TV. The doorbell broke my attention.

It was my maid. I didn't ask her for reasons, but she started elucidating her reasons for being so late.

"Saab, *maafi*! I was late because of my husband. Because today is a Sunday, he didn't go out for his work and was doing *nautanki*." I listened to her without saying anything. And after a few minutes, she again said, picking up broomstick kept on the corner of room. "You will be hungry. I will cook food," and she turned to clean the room.

I remained in the room till the evening. Maid left the house soon after cooking food. I was not in a mood to go outside, so after walking many times from the room to the balcony and back, I finally sat on the couch. It was true that I was silent and it happens to me when something bothered me. And it was true.

In the evening, brooding over something nonsensical and fuming over office work and colleagues, I felt hungry. It was a habit for me to eat something on a regular interval, either some snacks or biscuits. And so, for this, I kept my kitchen stocked. After taking a few biscuits from the kitchen and a can of cold drink, I lay on my bed. I decided to call my mother; usually, she called at this time, but without waiting for her, I dialled her number. After three rings, she picked up my call. "Hello mummy!"

"Chhotu! How are you? I was about to call you, and you called. Papa was also saying the same thing."

"I am fine. Office work is usual. Did Radhika call you?" I asked.

"No, she called yesterday. She didn't call you either?"

"No, I tried to reach her but her phone was unreachable.

After some time, I kept the phone down. Talking to my mother soothed me a bit. I kept my phone below my pillow and stretched myself under the bed sheet. I soon fell into heavy sleep.

It was almost 2'o clock when I had a dream, which first gave me discomfort, though I couldn't identify clearly, it soon it took over me, shook my strength. And soon, it started spreading slowly but soon fiercely and I was overtaken by the ferocious dream. When it reached its height, and I was experiencing a grief, a torment of infinite capacity, I woke up.

It was a dream, a vague dream. I saw a silent lounge and I was rushing for something. For what, I couldn't see in the dream.

My countenance was not normal; my shirt was wet with sweat. Suddenly I cried and then there was silence again. A foreboding silence. An evil one. I looked around. No one was there. It seemed that I stood in the middle of an ocean, and around me was water, just water, ready to drown me anytime.

Sweat appeared on my face even though the air conditioner was on, working properly, cooling the room.

I stayed in the same position for some time and then glanced at my phone. It was showing around 2:30 a.m. on the screen. A constant stream of dreadful images was swirling across my mind from one to another like a frog jumping. Turbulent, but disastrous. I switched on the table light kept beside my bed and in its flickering, not so dense light, I sat beside the lamp. I looked aimlessly at its bulb. But after a few minutes, I got up and started strolling across the room, taking some sips of water.

I came back to the bed, but was haunted with a chill and unearthly foreboding; I couldn't sleep. A number of times I adjusted my legs, tried different sleeping postures, adjusted the pillow, sometimes folded into half to make it thick, aligned myself in different angles, even spread the bed sheet on my body, but not a single attempt satisfied my impatience and anxiety. Counting minutes, and hours, I spent all night. In between, I even walked twice around the room.

I kept going back to the dream that had been haunting me. What could it mean? I didn't know. I pondered over this, but remained clueless. It had worried me so much that even today, after almost three years, I remember the dream exactly, without missing anything.

I carefully observed Randhir's expressions of fear and confusion, nodded and leaned back on the sofa. There was something about his way of speaking that bothered me. And each time he finished a sentence, there was tiny but meaningful silence left behind, a pain of unknown intensity that he tried to bury forcefully beneath the loads of emotions. I knew another person who did that. Naina.

I turned towards the bed. Looking at the star-filled sky, my memories wandered through the streets that led me to my home again, but for something cute and naughty this time. I drowned in my reverie once more.

I was sitting idle in my room, just looking at some vague things outside. It was evening and the sun had almost set on the other side. My buzzing mobile phone shook my attention. It was of Naina.

"Hello," I said.

"Hi, Akshat. What are you doing? Are you free?" she asked.

"Nothing great. Yeah, I am free," I said, wondering. "Why?"

"Actually, we all are planning to go shopping. Can you also come? We will have fun," she said. I heard the noises of others on the phone.

"Yeah, sure. I am also feeling bored here. Just give me two minutes. Where are you guys?"

"That's great. You just come to my place. Then we will go together," she said and disconnected the phone.

I changed my trousers and threw a fresh t-shirt on. I inspected myself in the mirror for the final time before I left the room, drove the car and reached within minutes to Naina's home. They were six of us. Two couples and then the two of us.

"Wow, great plan," I said, coming out of the car. Naina walked towards me, smiling. "So all of you are ready?"

"Yeah, we were just waiting for you. But how will the six of us go in your car?" Nimmi asked.

"You four go in the car and Nimmi, you come with me on the bike," Vikram said. Nimmi was his girlfriend.

"That's cool," Naina said. Without wasting another moment, we headed towards the mall. When we reached there, the two couples left us to go shopping. I was left with Naina.

"Shall we eat something? I am kinda hungry," I asked her.

She nodded. "What would you like to eat?"

"Anything you wish," she remarked.

I thought for a moment and said, "Shall we eat chicken pizza?"

She didn't say anything. And then I suddenly remembered that she was vegetarian. "Oh, I mean cheese pizza."

"No, you eat chicken pizza and I will eat some cheese pizza," she said.

Then we headed towards Pizza Hut. After coming out from there, she asked, "Do you have to buy something?"

"Not really. Why? You have to?" I asked.

"Yeah, but I can't buy with you."

"Why so? What is it that you can't buy with me?" I was surprised at her answer.

"Nothing, I can't tell you. Do one thing. Why don't you buy a t-shirt or something for yourself?" she said.

"Okay, I will go and just wander around. If you finish your personal shopping, text me," I said.

She nodded mutely. This was the first time she had said no to me. But I didn't mind it.

I wandered around the stores, tried several t-shirts but liked none of them. So I declined my idea to buy anything. I had enough clothes, and they kept gathering dust in my almirahs. It was around half an hour later when she texted me.

"I am in the Levi's showroom. Come over."

When I reached there, she was looking for tops and jeans. She picked up a top, glanced at it, and shook her head disapprovingly and kept it back. I watched her for several minutes before I walked over to her some newly designed tops and jeans. The shops had barely any customer and only sales person were also busy in counter, checking accounts.

"Try these," I said. She turned back to me.

"Oh, you have come," she said and looked surprisingly at the tops and jeans I was holding.

"You chose this for me?"

"Yes, I saw that you were trying hard to pick some good clothes but you were not able to. I liked these. Why don't you go try them out?" I said.

"Oh, sure," she said. Whenever I did something for her, she always looked at me cutely, admiring me, without saying. Before she went further, I pulled at the bags she was holding.

"Now, I am gonna check what you brought in my absence," I teased her.

"No, Akshat!" She frowned.

"Why not! What's so secret in shopping? I am not going to give this back to you without looking," I said.

"No, I said no," she said and leaped towards me to pull the bag out of my hand. But I was more alert than that. I just swung the bag to the other side. Next moment, her calm posture indicated that she had decided to let me check what was inside.

I put my hands inside the bags, looking into her eyes, sniggering. I saw that her face was devoid of expression. But I kept smirking. I felt clothes.

"Why were you not showing? It's just clothes," I said and pulled the clothes out. Seeing them, she felt embarrassed and avoided looking into my eyes.

When she did this, my curiosity increased, and then I looked at the clothes.

"Sorry," I grimaced and threw the clothes on the floor. *Undergarments! That too red, pink, black.*

I felt very embarrassed, turned my eyes to the other side, and handed the bag over to her. "I am sorry."

"Happy?" she remarked, with her stern voice. She sat down, picked up those clothes and put back into the bag.

"I didn't know. You should have told me, at least," I said, trying to defend myself.

She continued in the same tone. "What should I tell you? That..." she stopped, and then said, "...you should understand."

"Okay, my bad. I am sorry," I said, looking at her. "Go and try these now." She pulled those t-shirts out of my hands impulsively.

She went for the trial.

Stupid, idiot, nonsense, I scolded myself. Till she returned, I was checking out some jeans for me. When she returned, I saw her in her new clothes. Black fitted jeans, tailored perfectly for her slender legs. The sandals she wore were a perfect match for the top she wore, which was also perfectly tailored for her body. While wearing these things, I guessed, she had opened her hair, which fell in waves around her shoulder.

"It's so perfect. What do you say?" I said. "Yeah, the fitting is good." She brought all the clothes I had picked for her.

We came out of that store. We still had an uncomfortable silence because of the incident. She was still feeling embarrassed. I was too but finally, I decided to break this silence. "You can text others to meet us downstairs. We will have ice-creams and then leave."

She didn't say anything but when I looked at her, after waiting for her reply, I saw that she was texting them. In the meantime, we passed by some perfume stores.

"I am thinking about buying a perfume. I am so confused about fragrances. Can you choose for me?" I asked.

"Hmm," she said. "They will be coming after fifteen minutes."

"Okay, I guess fifteen minutes is more than enough to buy a perfume," I said and entered into the store.

Well, I didn't put any effort in choosing the perfume. I just looked at her. She was opening the bottle, pulling it close enough to her nose, smelled it, and then wait for a few seconds to realize its fragrance. I was curiously looking at her. It was amazing to see her this way. After smelling ten bottles, I guessed, she finally chose one for me. I paid and came out of the store, then headed downstairs.

Others were waiting for us, with lots of bags hanging down their arms. Lots of shopping, I gathered. We ate ice-creams. When the time came to pay bills, everyone was looking at each other, wondering who was going to pay. It seemed that everyone was out of cash because of that excessive shopping. I paid the bill in the end. Then we headed towards home. It was a lot of fun, though a brief embarrassing episode with Naina still floated in my mind. I looked towards her in the car; she was not looking at me, was gazing outside, lost in her own thoughts. I guessed her thoughts were about the clothes, too. I smiled.

13

Some Feverish Clues

She was back from Jammu and all else went on. It is several months later when I had come home from office in the evening. It was my salary day, so while coming back home, I packed up dinner as a surprise for Radhika.

I ordered all the favourites dishes of Radhika. I checked the time.

When I reached home, she opened the door. But her smile was missing, so was her lively expression.

"Hey, how was your day? I have already packed up the dinner. So no cooking today," I said and moved in to change the clothes.

Without saying a word, she left and kept the dinner bags in the kitchen. It was a bit surprising to me as she always used to sit with me and have a chat about the day.

So, I went to check where Radhika was. I found her in the bedroom, lying down.

"Radhika, are you okay?" I asked.

"Hmm," came a short reply.

Sensing something wrong, I moved closer to her and sat beside her.

"What happened? Aren't you feeling well?" I asked worriedly. She opened her eyes.

"Have a headache since morning… ever since you left for office," she said, holding my hand.

"You took medicine? Why didn't you call me? Let me take you to a doctor. Dear, this is pregnancy time. The baby is due in another month. We have to be very careful. I am thinking of applying for leave for one month till our baby comes into this world," I said, placing my fingers across her belly. "Aww, he or she is kicking you. Such a bad baby; giving pain to the mother."

She smiled but faintly. In the last few days of pregnancy, I bought a lot of toys, decorated a small room for the arrival of our baby, and coloured the walls in vibrant colours to give a jovial mood to the room. I glued several posters of cute babies everywhere. Cars, horses, Barbie dolls, everything, not knowing whether it will be a baby boy or baby girl. Even put a small cradle. Radhika was excited over my preparation. Although she was not allowed to walk or do anything, she sneaked around and watched me doing all this so excitedly.

"You were in a meeting. You remember, in the morning you said that you have a very important meeting with your foreign clients for which you have been preparing for the past one week. So, I didn't call you."

"Oh, I am sorry. Did you call the doctor?" I asked her. Impatience edged my tone.

"No, it seems fine now."

I felt relieved hearing this. I went back to the conversation of the same morning. I had told her about this meeting in the morning.

"Radhika, today, I have a very important meeting over an investment project. You remember, for the past one week, I was working on that project. You know, if I complete this deal successfully, I will get one bonus two-week Europe trip for free," I said.

"Oh, wow! And you know what, I am very sure that you will get it," she said, keeping the plate before me. "How many toasts would you like?"

"Four is enough. Where is your plate?" I asked, looking at her. It was only a cup of tea.

"Yes, I will eat. Let me finish this tea first," she said smiling.

"No, you know I can't eat without you. Please bring your plate otherwise all you will eat is one toast. Don't you care about our baby?" I said.

"Okay, okay," she rose and as she stepped towards the kitchen, I pulled her towards me and sat her down on my lap.

"Oh, what are you doing? Why are you pulling me?"

I always loved when she would to sit on me. She put her hands around my neck and started looking into my eyes. Looking deep into her eyes, my face glowed, and I said after a minute, "Give me a kiss." She kissed lightly on my left cheek. "No, on my lips."

She came closer, and our lips were merely at a distance of two millimetre. Her perfume filled my nostrils, filling me with pleasure. My arms went around her waist and hugged her tightly and I put my lips over her. I lightly ran my fingers over her lips, transferred over her cheeks. Whenever she was close to me, along with me, beside me, my face bloomed like a rose.

"Okay, now let me listen what our baby is saying," I said and brought my ear closer to her stomach.

"What is our baby saying?" she asked, moving her fingers through my hair.

"Sshh, our baby is saying something. But it's in some other language."

"What?" Radhika started laughing at my innocence.

"Don't laugh. May be our baby wants something from us before she or he comes into this world. We will fulfil our baby's every wish. Ok, hush. Let me hear," I acted like I was listening very intently.

After few moments, Radhika asked, "What is it?"

"Baby is saying how eagerly my papa and mummy are waiting for me to come in this world," I said and kissed her belly. "What will be his or her name? Have you decided on it?"

"Yes, I have decided our baby's name," she said excitedly.

When I raised my eyebrows in surprise and she said with a smile, "Tamanna if it's a girl and Akshat if it's a boy."

"What? Akshat? It's my name," I said.

"Yes, Akshat. Your name."

After that, she continued telling me her dream, about a happy and contented life and to live in a house in Patna. But when I showed my disagreement over the city, she gleefully agreed that she will live where I will live, so we can be together forever. I always smiled at her childish dream but it also filled me with undefined happiness. She always said that our house would be lively with the crackling of children; it would have a balcony from where she will see me off to work and that she would cook chicken for me in the kitchen while I would take care of our children.

I knew that motherhood is one the happiest moments for any women, and Radhika was so happy about this. Me too. But...

With that but, his face started twitching into something different. His eyes suddenly closed, his nose and mouth drew in, his jaw twisted to the side and it seemed that words were not able to come out of his mouth.

But it never happened…She never became a mother. It was a miscarriage.

It began in a way I had never imagined. With the passing of days, our love blossomed in a great way; I would start feeling restless if I didn't hear her voice for more than two hours. Either I sent a message or gave her a call every hour to hear her voice. Every time, I came up with a new way to talk to her: either to ask something and call her so she couldn't doubt why I kept calling her so often. Most of the time, I called her to let her know that I might be late in coming home in the evening, although on those days I reached home early to surprise her. She used to ask why I had called about being late. To hide my lies, I would always reply in a calm tone, that the meeting got over early. Sometimes, I called her to know what she was doing or if she needed something to be bought on my way back home. I knew she hardly asked me to bring something from the market and her reply remained a no, but I eventually ended up buying something while returning home.

That day, I had to go for a meeting in Mumbai. It was a day-long meeting and I had to return back the next morning. Before meeting, I called in the morning to know what she was doing. At that, she said that she was watching TV. In the noon, I had a meeting with the top banker of my bank. It was supposed to last for more than three hours. So, I decided to call her and inform her. I called her three times, but she didn't pick up the call. I was completely clueless, and then I realized that she might be in the bathroom or kitchen. I came back to the meeting hall. While the meeting was in proceeding, I called several times but every time there was no answer.

Every single moment was restless. I felt impatient to hear about her, about her condition. I had never been worried like this before.

As the meeting got over, I rushed towards the airport. There were one more meeting to held, but I skipped that.

It was around 8:30 p.m. There was still two hours to pass before the flight take off. I was strolling impatiently around the waiting room, calling her regularly, waiting eagerly to hear her voice, to know her condition. Somehow, two hour passed. She gave me a missed call around 11 p.m. I hurriedly called her back.

"Hello, Radhika. How are you? What happened to you? Is everything alright?" I asked a series of questions, my impatience and restlessness was not yet over.

"I have some weakness and due to which, a little fever," she said. Her sound was coming slow, barely coming out of the throat. It was a fragile and feeble voice.

"Weakness? You never care for yourself and you also don't listen to me. Listen, take some juice. Pomegranate juice. It's good for health and also help in blood formation. Eat fruits. Did you eat something? Have you taken medicines?" I said, hysterical. Listening to her voice relieved me a bit, just a little bit.

"Randhir, how much you care for me! I had my dinner. I also took the medicines. The fever will subside, don't worry," she said. "Did you take your dinner?"

"No, leave it. You still have fever?" I ignored her questions and replied.

"Randhir I asked you something. I know you didn't take your lunch too. And now dinner?" she was not in the mood to leave this.

"I was worried about you. How would I eat without knowing your condition? You are suffering from fever and I should eat?

How is this possible? Now that I know you're fine, I will eat," I said slowly.

"I love you, I love you very much. No one cares for me like you do," she said, affection and love gripping her tone. Her tone was still fragile, and I was worried for that. "I still have fever, 103 degrees."

"Oh, my god! This is too high. And you are telling me now. You take rest. Doctor advised you to take rest. I will call you again. Sleep properly. Cover yourself in a blanket. Do one thing, take two blankets."

"Room heater is working. I am not feeling cold. Now, don't worry about me and you also go and sleep. Two blankets!! Do you want me to suffocate and die?" she asked teasingly.

"Just shut up. And do say such words again. You only think about yourself. What would happen to a soul without a body? What would happen to me without you? Never use such words," I blurted out, and then used a more normal and slow tone.

"I am sorry. I didn't mean that. I am fine, dear. Now, smile and go to sleep." Again, her tone caught the same frequency, same tone of cuteness.

I hurriedly disconnected the phone, aboard the plane.

Food was not passing down my throat; I was barely able to eat half a roti.

As the airplane landed, I rushed home. I had to ring the bell a countless times before she opened the door.

Her face was pale. Her hair was untied and bleary eyes clearly confirmed that something was wrong.

"Radhika, are you fine?"

"Still feverish."

Just closing my eyes slowly, I said a prayer, asking God to make her well and healthy soon. I couldn't see her like this. I couldn't remember when I had prayed the last time. I was strolling in the room. Time was passing slowly, and my impatience was increasing rapidly.

"How is she feeling now? Would the fever have reduced?" I thought and touched her forehead. It wasn't that hot now.

After an hour, and on repeatedly touching her forehead, she woke up, said in drowsy and fragile tone, "Randhir, I am well. You didn't sleep yet. I will be okay. Fever is down now."

"Radhika, I am not feeling sleepy. You sleep. I am here beside you," I sensed her drowsiness. "You sleep." And I pulled the blanket till her neck.

Little relief, I felt. I lay on the bed, trying to sleep but I couldn't succeed. I was staring constantly on the watch.

Suddenly, when I heard some fragile voice of Radhika, it aroused me from my sleep. I went and splashed water on my face. Water was cold enough to numb my face. I shivered.

Sleep evaporated soon after.

"Radhika, how are you feeling now?" I asked.

"It's too hot. I am sweating now. I don't want to cover myself in the blanket. Room heater is also working. Fever is fully down," she said, annoyed.

"No, Radhika, you are not going to put off the blanket. Cover yourself for two more hours. Till then, you would be fully okay," I said in little authoritative tone.

"But Randhir, it's very hot and I am sweating a lot," she protested.

"Sweating is good for fever. Come on, cover yourself."

"Tell me ten times that you love me and give me a sweet and

lovely kiss, not one, more than a thousand times, and I would be fine in a second. That is the better, not better but the best medicine for me instead of this foul-smelling syrup and tablets," she giggled. This was the first time I saw her saying something so openly. Joy flowed out within me.

"Why a thousand? Millions times is good. Isn't it?"

She chortled, "How sweet! Okay, I am closing my eyes. Give me a kiss and don't cheat."

I planted a kiss on her forehead.

"You know Mr. Verma, our neighbour, was shouting at her wife that her mother is not going back home. It has been many months."

I laughed. "From where did you hear this?'

"I was in the balcony when I heard this. His wife was in no state to say anything. She was just trying to make him remember that his father stayed here for two months. Then both started arguing with each other, screaming at each other."

I broke into laughter on hearing this. "That is really funny. That's the problem when a family starts living nuclear and with time, they don't want to see each other's parents."

"Seriously," she giggled at my comment. After so many hours, I heard her giggle and it relieved me a lot. And then just as suddenly, she vomited blood.

"We are going out for a movie today. Evening show. Are you coming?" Nimmi asked Naina.

"No, yaar. I have to visit Akshat. He wasn't in college even today," Naina said.

"Why? What happened? Is everything fine?" Riddhima asked.

"I don't know. I tried calling him but he is not responding to calls."

"Then why don't you call his other landline number?" Vikram asked.

"I don't like calling there much. I better visit his home. You guys go and enjoy," she said.

"Okay, if he is fine, then you both also join us," Vikram said.

"Yeah, sure." Naina made a short reply as her mind was thinking about my condition. She left for my house.

"Driver. Please drive directly to Akshat's house," Naina said, sitting in the rear seat.

"But ma'am, have you forgotten that Saab ji said to drive back to home directly. Saab ji was saying you have to go to some party," the driver said, without turning back, looking at her through the mirror.

"Oh shit! I forgot," she murmured. After pondering for a moment, she said, "Yeah, I remember now. You do one thing. First drive to Akshat's house. It's just a two-minute work. Then we will go straight home."

"Okay," he made a curt movement of the head, but then he drove the car.

After reaching my home, she hurriedly opened the car gate and ran towards my room, shouting, "Just two minutes."

On entering home, she was greeted by my cook. "Hello, Naina ma'am. How are you?"

"I am fine," she said and without extending the conversation, she asked, "Where is Akshat? He was not in college today?"

"Oh. He is quite unwell since morning. Now, after taking medicine, he is sleeping in his room," the cook said.

"What?" she said, "But he didn't tell me anything. Did he consult the doctor?"

"Yeah, the doctor just left. I guess an hour earlier," he said.

"Why so late?" she was baffled at their negligence.

"You know, ma'am. Did he ever tell anything to anyone? I was fortunate enough that I saw that the door was open. So, I thought he has bunked college. When I entered the room with lunch, I found him sleeping. I called out two or three times. But when I didn't get any response, then I got suspicious about his health. So I checked his body temperature. And it was so hot that I was so scared. Then I called the doctor."

"Oh, god! Why didn't he tell anyone? He doesn't even tell me. I am going to scold to him a lot," Naina said. Her face had the shadows of both rage and care. After speaking her words, she left for my room.

On entering the room, seeing me sleeping, her emotion of rage melted within a second. I was sleeping, covered with a blanket.

She came, sat beside me and checked my body temperature. It was still hot. Then suddenly, she remembered that her driver was waiting for her. So, she rushed towards the gate. Driver was outside the car, chewing his nails.

"Ma'am, you took so much time. Let's go. We are getting late," he said and opened the door of the car.

"Akshat's health is not good. So, I won't be able to go. His mom and dad are not also home," she said.

"But ma'am, saab ji is waiting..," he couldn't even complete his sentence before Naina interrupted.

"Do one thing. Tell papa that I was not willing to go to the party as I have lots of assignments and project work to be completed and I am doing those with Akshat. I have duplicate keys for my home. Or, if I really need something, I will call Papa."

"Okay, ma'am," he said unwillingly and left.

Naina came back to my room. I was unaware of her presence till midnight when I woke up for water. I was feeling very thirsty and was covered with sweat, was feeling hot. So I pushed the blanket aside. The light was switched off. I smelled some fragrance, quite familiar to me and asked, "Naina, is that you?"

"Yes," she said and switched the light on.

I looked at her. It was still surprising to my eyes that she was in my room at this time.

"What are you doing here?" I asked, trying to sit, leaning against the bed. "I guess it is quite late."

"Oh, Akshat. Don't try to sit. You are not well. You need rest," and she pulled the blanket back on me.

"You didn't answer my question."

"Is that more important than your health?" she said, deliberately avoiding my question. "Water?" she brought me a glass of water. "Are you feeling hungry? I have food too." She said, indicating towards the plate of food.

Seeing her care, my eyes filled with tears of gratitude. "Yes, I am starving. Let me wash my hands."

"Oh, don't get out of the bed. I will feed you," she said, and brought the plate and sat beside me.

She took a piece of chapati and put it inside my mouth. After Daima, she was the first one to have cared for me with such genuine concern. While eating, she said, "I came in the evening. You were not responding to my phone calls. So, I came to see if you were here. Then your cook told me that you are not well. So, I decided to stay here. Even your mom and dad aren't home. You never tell anything to anyone. Not even to me." Saying the last words, she lowered her voice. "I know you don't even trust me."

"Hey, it's not like that. I trust you. I don't know when I got sick

and fell asleep. Now cheer up," I said. "I know you also didn't have your dinner. Let me ..." I took a bite of chapati and put inside her mouth. She chuckled and that made me smile.

"Are you feeling good now?" she asked.

"Yes, but a little bit of weakness," I said, drinking the water.

"Take some medicine for that. And sleep again. I am pretty sure that you will feel good before morning," she said, pulling my cheeks. She rarely did this to me. And whenever she did this to me, I felt immense pleasure within me.

"I would say that you also take leave. You mom and dad would have been waiting for you," I said to her, lying down on the bed again and pulling the blanket over me.

"Oh, yes. Don't worry about that," she said, smiling.

"You are very sweet," and I dozed off within a minute.

Next morning, I woke up. The fever had almost gone and I was feeling far better. I didn't find her in the room and assumed she had left.

When I came near the washbasin, I found a few sticky notes on the mirror. I felt so happy that she knew that I surely would go to the washbasin, and had glued the notes on the mirror.

"Dear, I left when you were in deep sleep, around 4' o clock." "My papa was calling constantly."

"I will call you in the morning. Take care."

A smile crossed my face. Leaving the toothbrush on the washbasin, I rushed towards the phone and dialled her number. After five rings, she received my call.

"Hello," I said.

"Hi," her voice was quite dull and it seemed that she was sleeping.

"I guess you are sleeping. You sleep for now and call me when you are fully awake."

"No, I wasn't sleeping. How is your health now?" she asked. Her voice was still very low.

"I am doing well now. Fever's gone. I will be at your home by 12," I said. "I know you are sleeping. Don't say that you are not sleeping."

She didn't say anything. I understood that she had again slept on the phone as I heard her deep breath on the phone. I disconnected the call.

14

When Disaster Knocked

I was frightened seeing her vomit blood.

"Radhika," I called. My voice contained fits of agitation, and fear was clearly visible on my face. I had never seen this. So sensing the situation, without delaying for any moment, I took Radhika in my arms and rushed towards the car. In between, I kept looking at her. She was howling with pain. Her face was red. I was quite scared to see her like this. Tears brimmed in my eyes seeing her in this situation.

Putting Radhika in the rear seat carefully, I hurriedly drove the car. Every moment was filled with restlessness and the weight of each passing moment filled me with anxiety. I kept glancing at her. She was sobbing with pain, and vomited once again. Blood again. Seeing this, I was too nervous and accelerated my car to full speed.

As I entered the hospital, I started shouting in helplessness. Few people ran towards me followed by some nurses who brought along a stretcher.

'What happened to her?" the doctor asked as he hurriedly came to us.

"I don't know. She was fine but a few minutes back, she

vomited and blood also oozed out." I said in a cracking voice. My face was taut with fear.

"Okay, we are going to have to operate over her. She is going to be fine," he tried to relieve me.

The compounder and nurses took her to the chamber for an initial check-up and instructed me to wait outside. I kept looking at her till she vanished from my sight. Tears already beginning to spill down my cheeks and I hopelessly sunk into a chair.

Several hours passed and I didn't hear anything from them. When it was unbearable to see this, I stopped a nurse to ask for information about Radhika.

"Excuse me?"

"Can I help you?" she said softly.

"Yes," I said in diminished tone. "I had brought my wife here two hours ago. Doctor said that everything will be fine. But I heard no news from them. Can you please check out? I am very worried. I love my wife so much. Please…"

"Yes, please give me a few minutes," she said but her tone lacked any sincerity. When she left me but went off in some other direction; my blood boiled, and I started shouting.

"Why are you not seeing the doctor? I haven't heard anything from them. I love my wife so much. I will not let anything happen to her." My voice rose shrilly, layered with agitation and anger.

Seeing this, every other person who was sitting on the chairs in the waiting area, or who was in the line to fill the form looked over at the nurse.

When the nurse vanished, took a turn into a corridor without responding anything, I was aflame in anger and rushed towards the reception.

"Why are you here? I am shouting that my wife is dying. Why is nobody responding?' I shouted.

"Just give me a minute. What's your wife's name?"

"Radhika Verma."

Such a long wait was really making me anxious, and some inauspicious images starting forming in my mind. It was the longest day of my life. In such a tense silence, I heard my own heart beating and my throat as well as face was strangely dry. I kept walking around here and there; then, from the corner of my eye, I saw the doctor.

I rushed towards him. He was accompanied by a few nurses.

"Doctor saab, how is my wife? What happened to her?"

"It was labour pain. But now she is fine," he said, then a brief silence and then added, "It was delivery time. She has delivered a baby."

"What? Wow. That means I am a father. Please tell me whether it's a girl or a boy. What wonderful news you have given doctor! I am so happy," listening to the doctor's words, I couldn't control my excitement and happiness beamed from my face.

"Please listen, Mr. Randhir There is something I should tell you," he said, lacking any excitement in his tone. "Please come to my chamber." And he walked. I just followed him.

"What is it, doctor? Is everything fine?" He didn't reply anything. I tried to match his pace of walking. He didn't utter a single word till he reached the office and sat on his chair.

"Please sit down," he said to me.

"What is the important news, doctor? Please tell me. Please tell me whether I am a father of baby boy or girl. I also want to meet my wife. She would be happy to know this."

"Mr. Randhir. I understand your excitement but I am sorry to say that everything is not fine. She has delivered a still born baby."

"What! What are you saying doctor? You mean the baby was born dead? How could this be possible?" my words broke.

"Please gather yourself, Mr. Randhir."

"But doctor, we had taken care of everything. Diet, health everything. How is this possible? Does she know about this?"

"It sometimes happens in spite of utmost care," the doctor said, keeping a tone of hope in his voice, but I knew it was not going to soothe me at that moment. He added, "There is something else that I need to tell you."

Hearing this, my face fell abruptly into stern lines. "What's that doctor?"

He took some moments. It seemed that he was framing the words within in his mind so that he could say what he wanted to say in the way he felt most appropriate. "Reports have come in. And I was just checking the report, when I came to know that something is wrong with them. To confirm, we did some more tests."

An unpleasant and heavy sensation sat in my heart and I just wanted to hear the doctor out. An air of deep and irredeemable gloom hung over us.

"Doctor, please don't increase my anxiety any further and say what you have to say." I knew I was showing eagerness from outside but deep within somewhere I was afraid to hear anything negative.

"I am sorry to tell you this," the doctor began, "but your wife has brain tumour."

Listening to this, my mind went blank. Tears rolled out of my eyes. It seemed that words had stuck inside the throat. It was still unbelievable for me. A ghastly whiteness spread across my face.

"Brain tumour! What! What are you saying?" I almost collapsed.

"Yes. She has a brain tumour. And it is also reason that she had a miscarriage. It complicated the pregnancy process. How it began to grow inside her brain, it is not possible to say. It is quite complicated and has affected the pregnancy too. Though it is in initial stages, it's really tough to live with it. Now, we have to take care of her very diligently because none of us know how it will behave in the upcoming days."

Listening to this, it seemed that my heart would come out of me. I was silent, pondering over his words. Then he added, "Mr. Randhir, at this moment, it is important how you convey to her that the child was born dead. You know how women are, especially in the case of their children. She might leave her husband but can't live without her baby."

"Yes, doctor. I know what you are saying but don't know how I will tell her this. I know she won't be able to hear this. She will break. How eagerly we were waiting for this child!" my voice grew sad. Words were barely coming out.

"Yes, I understand that but you have to take care of this. It is very crucial for her health too."

I nodded mutely. "But doctor. Will she be okay? This disease is curable, right?"

"We have checked it up thoroughly, and this tumour is in its initial stage. We will do our best to cure this disease." His word assured for that moment but his voice lacked hope.

"How is she now? I want to meet her. I want to see her right away."

"She is sleeping for now. Once she wakes up, you can meet her."

"Yes, doctor. Do whatever you can do. I really love her. I can't live without her," my words were fragmented and I could only speak after many attempts. I could not help myself and I broke down, "How will I tell her this? I know she won't be able to take it."

"Please take care, Mr. Randhir." The doctor held my hand to supported me. "Please take care of her. Never leave her alone. Spend time with her. Try to keep her happy in whatever way is possible."

I nodded mutely but deep within my heart, I knew she was not going to be able to handle this. I thought about the whole preparation we had done for welcoming our baby into our world. The toys, posters, furniture, everything.

It bothered me. I asked myself several times how I was going to tell her all this? After many attempts, when I couldn't think about it, a queer, uncomfortable perplexity started invading me.

My tears were continuously rolling down thinking about all these things. How our beautiful dreams had taken a turn we had never expected.

"Oh, god. Why did you do this to us? We were so happy in our life. Can't you bear us being happy?" I muttered, covering my face with both palms. Then after some moments, a woman's voice broke my thoughts.

"Mr. Randhir?"

I uncovered my face and looked at her. Tears still had me cheeks wet. It was a nurse.

"Your wife is awake and is asking about you. You can meet her now," she said in a very normal tone.

"Hmm, thank you for informing me," I said and walked towards the room.

I stopped just before opening the door. I couldn't understand how I was going to say this to her but I opened the door and entered the room anyway.

She was on the bed, covered in a white sheet. The oxygen bottle was hanging on a stand nearby. She had closed her eyes but she wasn't sleeping. The air conditioner was running low as the temperature inside the room was quite normal. I walked slowly towards her and stopped near her face. My eyes were red and wet and my tears had dried. It had lost every emotion but I didn't want her to see me in this way, so I tried to keep a fake smile over my face.

I glanced over her face – serene, unaware of the storm that had just shaken our very being. Her face showed how much pain she had endured. Seeing her, tears started rolling down my face. I wouldn't be able to say anything to her. How could I?

I placed my palm over her face and with my touch, she opened her eyes. She held my hand.

"How are you feeling?" I asked. "You know, Radhika, after coming into my life, everything turned out so beautifully that I can't even describe it through words. I don't know how to say all those feelings. When you were not in my life and when I compare both lives, it seems that how things have turned out. Earlier, I never had thought that living with someone like you would make so much difference. There were some uneasiness about marriage but now, when I think about it, it seems hard to believe that I ever thought like this."

She was listening to me without blinking her eyes. "Randhir, where is our baby? Is it Akshat or Tamanna?"

I deliberately avoided her question and continued, "I love you, Radhika. I am who I am because of you, because of your love, care and am really happy about the life we have led so far. You are my reason to smile, every hope and every dream and I know that no matter what is happening or will happen in future, we will live it together. Won't we?" saying all these things, my eyes filled with tears and big drops plopped down my cheeks.

"I love you too, Randhir. Where is our baby? And why are you crying?" she asked, seeing my tears. She sat up against the bed. "What happened? Why are you not telling me anything?"

I drew myself closer to her and embraced her. I was almost on the verge of breaking down into tears but I knew that I had to be brave, or I won't be able to handle her. Embracing her, I said, "Nothing, Radhika. Everything will be alright."

"Why are you saying this again and again? Why are you not telling me about our baby?" she asked, but now her tone rose. "What happened to our baby?"

"Nothing, my baby. Nothing. Everything will be alright," I clutched her tightly.

"What will be alright? Please tell me where is our baby, Randhir? I want to see our baby. Please, please Randhir," she started sobbing. She put her palm on my face and asked, "Where is our baby?'

I wiped her tears. "Don't cry, baby. Our baby…" After many attempts, I too broke down but soon, I recovered myself.

"What, Randhir? What is this all about? Why are you not saying anything to me? Our baby is safe and healthy, right? Please tell me. You are scaring me like this."

"Due to some pregnancy complications, it was still born," I said with a heavy heart.

She remained silent. A ghastly whiteness spread over her cheeks. And suddenly she collapsed into hysterical crying. When

I heard her crying, my mind stung a thought. It was the same sound with the same pitch that I had heard in my dream. The same scream, a painful scream. The silence of the hospital and the upcoming storm of our life. It matched with my dream sequence. The air of gloom that hung all over the place also matched with the gloominess of my dream.

There was not a single moment when she didn't cry over the lost child. For a month, I had taken leave from office to take care of Radhika, based on the doctor's advice. I was also very sad but I didn't let my feelings surface in my demeanour in any way, for otherwise I wouldn't be able to hold her, support her. It was really tough for me. Every time I put her to sleep, I used to think about her pain. That's true that I couldn't feel the same way that she felt for being un-mothered. She had lost interest in everything, was not even eating properly. When her desperation and sadness grew wilder, she asked me, "Randhir, where is our baby?" She said she wanted to hold him. She would say, "I know he would have possessed the same chiselled face, the soft pink lips, and the long nose as you. I want to feel the softness of his cheeks, small ears and wondering eyes, trying to understand the world. His gleeful smile." Whenever she did this, the only thing I could do at that time was to nod, keeping her hands in mine, whispering consolations to her, made her believe that she would conceive once again and this home would fill with sounds of joy. For a moment, when she stopped sobbing, looked at me with a faint smile, and closed her eyes, I would think it relieved her, but the next moment, her desperation grew wilder and made me break into tears. Human emotions are hardly relieved by anyone's support or care. Care and support relieves someone for just about a few moments. It was the same with Radhika. Her longing for a child, a desperation which sometimes grew so wild that the whole night was spent in making her feel comfortable, singing lullabies to make her sleep. Sometimes, it was successful, but most of the time, it was not. With time, she started losing her mental control and behaved in very unusual ways which brought nothing but tears of helplessness in me.

During the day, for hours and hours, she kept staring at the room which we had planned for our child. She went inside, tried to sit over the small scooter, chuckled at me, and said, "This is how our baby will sit and we will push him from behind together." I tried to smile, crying within my heart, as I looked at her. She nudged me, motioning my sight towards the small mosquito net and said in squeaking tone, "See, this is such a cute, small mosquito net for the baby. But I will never put the baby under this alone. I will nestle our baby to my chest the whole night. Who knows when he will need something. You never know. Assume the baby sleeps in that net in this room and needs me. And I slept here and if he cries in the middle of the night, then who will take care of him? No, I won't let my baby cry. I have to understand his needs. Water. Milk. I will give my own milk. You know doctors say it is healthy for the baby." Listening to this, and seeing her face, I broke into tears and left the room. I didn't want to cry in front of her. Her heath condition kept deteriorating. Whenever I used to give her medicine, she would ask innocently, "What is this for? Would this medicine give our baby back?" I would nod, and sometimes tears streamed down my face, seeing her in this condition.

When she remained normal, from time to time, she would call out to me, "Randhir?"

I would put down whatever work I was doing, and looked at her with a smile.

She would smile back and say, "Nothing."

And I would start working again.

When she kept repeating my name, I would leave my work and come to sit beside her, run my fingers through her hair. She would look at me for a few moments, eyes filled with lots of things to say, but avoiding them, and she would rest her head on my shoulder, hold my arm and start sobbing.

Almost every night, it happened that to soothe her feelings, I would hug her, make her sleep on the bed. It had been very long since I had slept properly. Whenever my eyelids used to drop, her desperation returned back, and I would have to wipe her tears, console her.

My world was falling apart. The bird which nested for the future had been shattered in the storm of life.

15

The Flight of Love

It had been a few months and I hadn't joined office yet. Phone calls from office asked for my attention. I tried my level best to manage my work from home, but I knew it couldn't have been dragged like that for too long. Soon after, I received a letter stating that I was being fired from the job. At that time, it really didn't bother me. I just wanted my Radhika back in my life. The same Radhika that I had fallen in love with.

"Radhika, it's time for your medicine, dear," I said.

"No, I won't take medicine. Why do you keep giving me these medicines? I have realized that you are giving me medicines for the last one month? What has happened to me?" she asked innocently.

"Nothing has happened, dear. Just a bit of health issues and the doctor has said that you will be fine pretty soon," I tried to relax her.

But it was not true. Her heath conditions had deteriorated with time. She had lost a lot of weight and her hair too was falling. Whenever she was sleeping, I used to cry alone. Her conditioned worsened one night; she vomited blood again. I was distraught looking at this. I hurriedly took her to the hospital.

167

When I saw her through the glass window, seeing her on the bed with an oxygen mask on her face, an overwhelming grief wrenched my heart out. An unsettling silence prevailed there.

I gathered some courage and walked into the room, "Randhir," Radhika said, clutching my hand. Her voice was so soft that I was barely able to listen. I went closer to her. She seemed so weak, her eyes sore, her lips dry, and it gave me a shiver.

"Hmm?" I said. "Radhika, you will be fine very soon. I can't see you this way." Saying this, I hid my face behind my palms so that she couldn't see me crying. I couldn't have afforded to break her courage at that time.

"Do you love me?" she asked in the same tone. Hearing this, I raised my head, looked at her. Her eyes were wet with tears, and I was in the same condition.

"I love you," I said. "Of course, I love you. My world would be barren without you, dear." I kissed her on the forehead. She drew a long breath. But something was bothering me. Why was she saying all this?

"Then, will you do something for me?"

"You know that I will. Why do you even have to ask," I could clearly hear my own voice, choked up due to the controlled tears. I held her hand in mine.

"Even if it's hard? Even if you don't want to?"

Her voice was too feeble to say anything. I put my fingers across her face and said, "Ask for anything and I will do it. Anything to keep you smiling. I can," I said but paused. "Radhika, what's going on? Why are you asking such things?"

She took a long, deep breath before answering. I was still puzzled over her words and they were still ringing in my ears.

She looked at me for a moment before she spoke, "I know it is a bit difficult for you, but can you live one day without seeing me?" I was beyond myself with shock and surprise.

"But why?" I said, "Once you get out of this bed and come back home, then I will live without seeing you. But for now, no, never!" And I tightened my grip on her hand, as if scared that she'd let go of it. She was adamant about her wish and unwillingly, and only to keep her word, I accepted her request.

I waited impatiently outside the room. Every second was a like a year. I spent the whole night walking, waiting for this examination of my life to pass. I wanted to go and see her. Twenty-three-and-a-half hours had gone.

After an impatient half-an-hour, the door opened. I hurriedly ran towards the nurses.

"Where is she?" I asked. But without any words, she handed me a letter.

My eyes quickly scanned the whole page and my eyes stuck to the top right end. The letter was addressed to me. I read the name and re-read it all over again. It was her handwriting. For the first time, some inauspicious feelings came across my mind that left me terrified. Why would she write a letter to me when she could have easily called me and talked? With trembling hands, I opened the letter. I held my breath and seeing the familiar handwriting, and reading the first words, tears rolled out. My heart was beating hard, I could hear my heartbeats in my ears, loud and clear.

My mind was tremulous, and the weather outside only echoed the storm in my mind. The wind outside was wild, with hammering rain and I shivered. The wind had become fiercer and the window panes were swinging uncontrollably.

She had left me the letter as her last message; she had gone forever and her ephemeral but enchanting beauty had expired forever, leaving me devoid of all things I had lived for."

As his words reached my ears, my muscles twitched and mind froze. I left everything as it was and turned towards him. I was stunned, as I tried to comprehend what he had said a minute earlier. He was looking into the fire, with a letter in his hand. A sense of bewilderment ran through my nerves like the chill of icy winds. I walked towards him, still not believing what he said.

My darling husband,

If the nurse has handed this letter over to you and you are reading this, I am sure I have passed on to the other world.

It was just the first two lines, and I was agape and was totally choked by a rising convulsion of grief. I shakily steadied myself on my feet. My lips trembled, my sight blurred as tears started rolling out of my eyes, my body froze and rivulets of sweat dribbled along the temple and it seemed that I had lost everything I had ever lived for. It seemed that my heart just burst out and the letter fell out of my hand. My world had broken down to bits and I couldn't even see a hope to gather it. Panic took over me. A glacial pang, like the stab of a dagger of ice frozen from a poisoned well.

Reading that, it seemed that my world that Radhika and I had created with so much care, my love, had shattered. My body was frozen; my heart throbbed at its highest possible speed, my hands grew limp. Eyes were dilated with feelings of anger, despair, betrayal and finally tears started rolling down. I didn't understand anything. I just stood like a statue. I wanted to say something, but what, how, I really didn't know. My mouth remained open with shock that started swirling through my nerves. Body temperature began to rise. I wanted to forget everything and just cry.

Hysterically, I clutched the nurse's arms and asked, "What is this? How could this have happen? No, she can't leave me."

With tears in her eyes, she whispered," I am sorry. She is no more in this world and she asked me to hand over this letter to you before she took her last breath." She sobbed. "I couldn't say anything to you as she had made me promise." Her tone hinted at the feeling of regret.

Leaving her, I ran towards the room and my feet just stopped moving when I saw her sleeping, in death. The oxygen mask was uncovered. And her face was covered with a white bed sheet. I sobbed, and crept in with heavy feet. My eyes were red, and sore. My hand trembled and I pulled away the bed sheet to look at her. Looking at her serene face, it seemed that tears would have no end that night. Words choked and tears were rolling out on the cheeks without measure. I looked at her, splayed my hand across her. I wanted to say something. But who was I supposed to say it to now? Nothing was left there except unwelcoming silence that was ready to eat me up, that would eat at me for the rest of my life.

I broke into cries holding her head close to my chest, "Radhika, you can't leave me. We have to live forever. You can't leave me. Open your eyes. I will never let you go away from me."

The scream of pain that escaped me brought with it a lifetime of silence.

I didn't know what to do. I had asked our parents to leave it to me to look after her, and I had failed. I had promised her that I would keep her happy, and I had failed. I had lost everything and I didn't know what to do. That's when I thought of the letter and went back to read the whole of it.

My darling husband,

If the nurse has handed this letter over to you and you are reading this, I am sure I have passed on to the other world. I am sorry. I asked the nurse to not say anything to you. The disease had eroded me and there was no chance left of survival. I knew you won't be able to see this. I know if I were in your position, it would have been equally hard for me, but I believe you were the stronger of the two of us.

I know how much you tried to keep the truth away from me that I had brain tumour and I won't be living for too long. You kept giving me medicines and innocently convincing me that I would be fine one day. But I think god has written this much of journey for the two of us together. It has ended. I read the medical reports in your absence one day. So I decided to write this letter.

You know very well how much I love you and would love to be your wife all through. I took time to understand you but once I came to know the real you, I found you the most romantic and caring husband. Yes, we had an arranged marriage but with the passage of time, our love blossomed and that really made my life special. In other words, you made my life special from the ordinary. We shared some beautiful times together and enjoyed every stage of our love. I have just one regret: I couldn't give you a child. Please forgive me for this. I never knew this would happen as I wished to live some more time with you. Always remember our wonderful days and please remember those moments with a smile. I will always be with you. I know it would be difficult for you but it would break my heart not to see you happy. Please do it for me. Though each moment shared with you was precious for me, but one moment, the night of our wedding and your uneasiness, still brings a smile to my face. There is still another world for you of which I was just a small part. So smile and keep working. Everything will be beautiful. And one more thing, the day that marks my passing away should not be a day to mourn. It should be a day for you to remember me and the love we shared. And if possible, visit Dehradun on my death anniversary every year.

I know your eyes would still be wondering about why I had asked you to not see me for one day, that too the very last day that I was left with. I am sure that you have fulfilled the promise. I also know that you wouldn't have budged from the door and would have sat all night near the door, waiting eagerly to see me. I also wanted to see you. It was not possible for me to die without seeing you. I wanted to take my last breath holding your hands together but I couldn't make myself that selfish. Please forgive me for this.

Dear, can I ask for one more favour? I know you will not let my last words go in vain. You spent a day without me. Can you spend all these years without seeing me? I know your tears have made this letter wet by now. I am sorry to hurt you, but now, I can die peacefully.

Thank you for everything, I am eternally grateful. I am always with you. Just close your eyes and feel me. Stretch your hands and I will be right there.

I am sorry. Please forgive me. I love you very much.

Love forever,

Radhika

Your honoured wife

As I finished the letter, I felt she had murmured all this to me. I became distracted, restless. My mind was blank and heart was beating unimaginably fast. The temperature was controlled but rivulets of sweat were flowing across my forehead, my temple. My feet seemed frozen and my voice choked inside my mouth. I didn't know what to say. I was aghast, face ashen and body seemed to have stopped reacting.

PART 3

16

After She Left

As he finished speaking, I directed my eyes towards him. He sat on the chair but was staring through the windows. I remained silent, waiting for his words but seemed lost in his own thoughts after that. The fire was bright and giving us warmth, keeping us safe from the cold weather outside. But what about the frozen feelings that he was fighting? Would the fire outside help warm this man up too, I wondered. I tried to see his face, but couldn't read his expression; his face was completely turned away from me. A few minutes passed in the same way and I couldn't find any suitable words to say or ask, so I remained silent. I couldn't understand anything out of this. I got up, and made my way through the room towards the balcony. Outside, the night was buzzing with the sounds of crickets. The moon had risen completely and was glowing in its full glory. I looked around, checked on the other side of the road. It was all silent. After staring into nothing, I settled down on the couch in the corner. The gentle light of the balcony sprung me back to life and reminded me of Naina again. A cold breeze picked up soon.

He stood, strolled towards the window and stretched his hands outside the window. I saw him closing his eyes, breathing deeply, taking in the softness of the rain. Silence followed his heavy voice and with the passage of time, his words started fading, yet fraught with emotions and with pain oozing out, he whispered, "It rained that night too."

When he left the fireplace, I was frozen to the same place. I read the letter. The body seemed paralyzed realizing the words and their meaning. He headed towards the room, and shut the door behind him. The thunderstorm was still heavy on the cottage, although it had become mild. The fire in the fireplace was flickering, seemingly in its last moments, which at last, drew my attention towards it. The wood had almost completely burned out and it would be extinguishing anytime now. Apart from the tapping of the rain on the window panes, and the intermittent lighting, the house was almost quiet like a graveyard. I didn't even realize when tears started streaming down my eyes too. With a sudden jolt, I just fell on the chair.

"How could be this possible? How could this have happened to such a nice person? The end had come all too soon." I said to myself. Maelstroms of emotions were storming inside my brain.

I reached the bed. This night was so terrible for both of us. Lying on the bed, I put to rest a fierce tide of feelings that again welled up within me. As I pondered over such questions, tears had no end tonight. I was mulling over this, and I pulled aside the curtains. The rain had almost stopped but there was no sign of stars in the sky. It was still dark with clouds. The stillness of everything was uncomfortable. I kept mulling over his words. Suddenly, Naina's face appeared before me. Her face, eyes filled with love for me. I sensed her touch, a touch full of care. In the next moment, I felt that Naina was sitting right in front of me, smiling at me. My heart filled with extreme love for her. I wanted to say to her everything that I had ever wanted to. I realized now that I also loved her. Naina, I love you. Then thunder again struck, and I didn't see her. She was nowhere. I rushed towards the place where she had been but couldn't find her. My mind remained blank. Then rain stopped and in a night of unfathomable blackness, where the sky was stained with the dark cloud, the moon slowly rose. A silver moon, like a new stamped coin, rode triumphant in the sky. A ray of happiness crawled on my face, a triumphant one. I realized that I had been dreaming. I understood her importance in my life. Now, I just wanted to go back and tell her everything. I didn't know whether she would accept me or not. You are my best friend, my shoulder to lean on, the one person I know I can count on, you're the love of my life, you're my one and only, you're my everything, I whispered to myself and drowned into a beautiful reverie. A beautiful and hopeful life stretched before me, alluring and refreshing as an open road. Realizing this, my heart filled with abundant joy.

I didn't know when I slept, but I was sure that it must have been early morning when I woke up. It was bright outside, and the air was cool. The rain had finally stopped. I glanced around. He had already awakened, was packing his bags. I looked at his face. It was quite normal, as if nothing had happened. I looked at him with admiring eyes and said to myself, how naturally he has masked his pain inside him.

"Good morning," I said.

"Oh, good morning! You have woken up. I was waiting for you to wake up," he said, pleasantly. For a moment, he looked at me but then, he again resumed his work, started packing clothes. Then he added, "Actually, I got a call from my office and we have to leave now. I am sorry that we have to hurry up like this."

"Why are you saying sorry? It's completely fine," I said and came out of the bed. "Let me pack up my bags too. It won't take much time. When do we have to leave?"

"I have called a cab already. He will be reaching within an hour. What's your plan after that?" he asked.

"I will go home," I said and smiled. He too smiled realising that I had made up my mind for good.

"If you don't mind, can I ask you something?"

"Yeah, sure," I said, wondering what he was going to ask.

"When I came to you room this morning, I heard your whisper some Nina's name, apparently in your dream."

When I heard this, I felt a bit embarrassed, "She is my best friend. And perhaps she loves me but I never pay heed towards her."

"You know what, it might be that you couldn't realize that so far. You can't realize sometimes who you love most. But, your eyes reveal what that person really means to you by crying for them. A similar thing has happened with you. Calling out to her in a state of emotional unrest is an example of this," he winked. After a moment, his face resumed the previous evening's seriousness.

"Yeah, I too realized that I love her. It's all because of you. Hadn't I heard your story, I couldn't have realized her love. I understood the meaning of love, the way to love anyone. You are absolutely right. If someone bad did something wrong with you, it doesn't mean love is a bad emotion. You know, she had said the same thing to me once, that one day somewhere I will realize this. Thank you so much." A radiant look came over my face like a sudden burst of sunshine on a cloudy day. He didn't say anything but the smile on his face said everything. "Now, I just want to go her as soon as possible and I would say everything that I have felt for her all this while. I don't know whether she will accept me or not but I would find pleasure in saying what I feel for her."

He heard me and then whispered, "Love comes into our life unannounced and to keep waiting for the right time is wasting away very precious moments. Don't wait anymore; just go ahead and say it."

I could just smile in agreement. He quickly added, "Yes, you will. And in a few minutes, the cabby will come."

"Yes, my bag is almost packed and I am also ready," I replied. Deep within myself, before leaving, I wanted to know what happened after that but I had no courage to ask him. I just thought that he had so much pain already in his life, I wouldn't increase it. If he felt good about it, then he might tell me what happened after Radhika's death.

I was true to my thinking and didn't ask him anything, and true to his spirit, he began telling me about the same suddenly.

It happened when we were in the taxi and both of us were silent, waiting for the other to initiate some conversation. He began in a way that didn't give me any hint that he would explore his past again.

"The weather is so fine. See! The blue bowl of sky has just been stretched with the luminous sun on the other horizon," he said, adjusting the window of his side, lowering the glass. "Akshat, just listen to the soft murmur of air on the tree-tops, rushing into the taxi. So soothing."

"Yes, it is."

"I just love this place." He made a short remark after a brief silence. I just looked at him. He tilted his head against the glass window, and took in the fragrant air.

"I love it too." But he remained as he was, unheeding my appreciation for this place. I noticed a change in his face that turned into a grave look as he said, "I wished I could enjoy a few more springs with Radhika here, but..." he stopped, seemed at a loss of words but gathering all his scattered strength to revive something, he spoke again:

"But it seemed that life had been arrested, as the horologist with interjected finger, arrests the beating of clock after she is gone. I lay awake for several nights after her demise, thinking that I can still hear her, and belying the fact that she had gone. My Radhika had gone to a place from where no one returns. I wished deep inside that it would turn out be an atrocious dream until the red streaks appeared on the horizon and a new day broke out, followed by the cranky sound of the alarm clock as there was no one to wake me up with a smiling face and say, 'Wake up, Randhir! I'll have your tea ready.'

"For the next few weeks, I stayed in the room, feeling forlorn and adrift. Disfigured by the monotony, I realized that I had to break the fortress of pain and sorrow to revive again the life that Radhika had asked and expected me to live. Though the cruel memories never shed their wings, in spite of this, I decided to embrace this very life from a different angle. Once I had an idea to shift to another apartment, but that I might betray the moments that these walls enclosed within them made me forget the idea. My bank balance was low and I was without a job.

"Over and over the paroxysm of grief and longing submerged me but I came out of sombre moods, momentarily, and applied for a job. Within a few days, I got a good job. I was qualified and experienced; that was not as difficult as I had imagined. Every time I returned from office, I stretched my hand towards the doorbell with the hope that I would see Radhika's smiling face. But before I could do so, my eyes got stuck on the iron lock hanging on the latch and I dropped my half-stretched hand.

"Each time I sat down in the dining room, I realised I was all alone to fend for myself. My mother had stayed me for a few weeks after this tragedy, but she could not see me in such sorrow so she asked me to gather courage and went back.

"Every morning, for several months, even sometimes now, I woke up, but sill closing eyes, I reached for her, to touch her shoulder, the sighting of her tousled hair, and the familiar feminine fragrance. But my hand found nothing, just emptiness. I realized her absence.

"This happiness, together with the look of appeal on that radiant face, was something that made my dishevelled morning state also something to look forward to. And it had been lost forever.

"Some memories would rise, unbidden, and there would be stony silences, eroding silences. Sometimes, it seemed that she might have woken up, so I called her in my dreamy tone, 'Oh, Radhika. You woke up so early. Please come and sit beside me. I want to keep my head in your lap.' When I didn't get any reply, I opened my eyes, looked around and observing the dreadful calmness around me. Tears slipped down my cheeks unchecked. 'Why have you left me, Radhika? Was my love so weak that we couldn't see the several years of spring together? How on this earth would I live with you? Was our journey just for this long?' And whenever feeling this, I nestled myself in the pillow with enormous pain in my heart, a soft voice started resounding in my ear, that was soothing, 'No, honey. I am with you. Not beside you, but within you: in your heart for ever. Can you feel me? Just close your eyes.'

"When I closed my eyes, my ears could hear the music of her breath."

I was struck with the intensity of this man's pain for his lost love. It felt like I had wasted such a lovely time with Naina by not being able to realise my love for her.

While I was lost, Randhir continued speaking, "I wanted to feel her, smell her and realize her and closing my eyes was the only way I could. I close my eyes every time I missed her immensely. I felt her sari pallu sweep across my face, I felt her around me. I understood that although she was not with me physically, but she was always with me. Whenever I did this, I never wanted to open my eyes. I knew, if I opened my eyes, the devastating silence that would welcome me, falsifying all the belief that I had felt so far of feeling her. At that time, my dream was far better than reality, and I always wanted to live there, with her.

"It still happened after a year. I came to the room after bathing, feeling fresh, energetic, and clean after a long sleep. I came to the dressing table and wore some scent, put on a pyjama and a t- shirt. My thought never wandered; it must have wandered hardly once over these years, over the presence of somebody, someone special, and someone close, my wife, with whom I could share everything. But today, I couldn't figure out how my mind wandered and I asked someone, someone who was not in the room, 'Can you please take care of tea and paper?'

"I kept looking into the mirror but turned back after a few minutes when silence prevailed all over there and found an empty room. My lips drooped and my heart sank. Memories got refined slowly. My handsome face took on a distracted expression. I understood that no matter how busy I keep myself, I would never forget her. She is me."

We both were silent. Then, for a moment, the rain stopped and a light wind outside the lattice swayed some branches of rose to and fro, shaking out their perfume.

"You might be wondering that what I was doing in Varanasi. The day we met was her second death anniversary. So, I was returning back from Varanasi after paying a tribute to her."

My tears were on the verge of rolling down.

He heaved a deep sigh and said in a voice choking with grief, "All sounds of song that we were singing together were lost in the whistle of air humming by. It felt like the flight of a million arrows that finally pierced me, stabbed me as ruthlessly as hoof of a horse tramples on a rose. It left me to live a life where I die every single day."

The courage he had showed me in the morning broke, and tears rolled down his face. I said looking at him, "Someone said it correctly that death ends just a life, not a relationship." But before I could have said any more words, at the same time, the driver pulled the brake and said looking into the mirror, "Station!" And my tears that I had been holding back for a long time, finally slid down.

We came out of the cab. He paid the fare. We moved ahead towards the platform.

17

Coming Home to Life

I boarded the train. Just before the train started whistling, he handed over an envelope to me and said, "Your ticket."

I took the envelope and smiled at him. A tear glistened at the corner of my eyes and whispered, "Thank you for telling me your story. If I know what love is, it's because of you." We exchanged our contact numbers.

He remained silent for a few minute, looked at me and said, "Go and live your life. There are no second chances."

I nodded. When the train signalled and honked its start, I waved at him. He smiled and reciprocated. Soon the train left the platform. I stood there till he went out of my sight.

I returned back to my compartment, settled on my seat and drew my curtains. Sitting idle for a few minutes and thinking of this remarkable man brought tears to my eyes as my mind was thinking about something else. To capture everything, I took out my dairy and began writing.

Some incidences of life change you in a way that cannot be undone. Some conversations and people associated with it last in your memory for a lifetime. I can say that this unexpected short trip of my life changed everything for me, forever. Randhir's conversation and his story left such a deep mark on my mind, provided answers for every possible question in my life. Now, I found meaning in everything. It filled me with relief, a fragrance of life which has an air of vitality and vigour. His story made me realize the importance of Naina in my life, the sweetness of her laughter, the innocence of her care and advice. It relaxed me.

I stopped for a moment, looked outside at the passing trees and the sun running with me. "Life always passes in the same way if we forget to remember where we are headed."

To me, Mr. Randhir predominantly is a man of passion, struggling through life while maintaining his virtues and different good qualities. A great soul hurt and scourged but still equipped with dignity. Even after he had experienced so much pain in his life, had suffered the loss of his wife whom he loves dearly and believes that she is still with her, beside him all the time, he sticks to a good life. I too had observed that in his dark eyes he eclipses the predominating infinite love for her. Though every single time he spoke, he tried hard to mask his agitation and grief. I sensed everything, a soft intonation of profound sorrow. How, I didn't know. Maybe living with him, spending time with him and listening to him, along with some sense of understanding the human psyche, had equipped me to read his thoughts. All emotions, and that one particularly, love, were abhorrent to me but now, everything turned out to be so beautiful, alive. When I look back, at myself seven days ago, I realized that something has changed inside, what I achieved in these days. Something that I could have never learnt from anyone, at least not from my parents. Sometimes, Naina also tried, not directly, to teach me something about it but I couldn't understand her. I have realized now that one should adore the one who gives you their time. Last night was really terrible, still brings shiver to my nerves when I think about it. But to falsify all the things, the way he presented himself, next day, was really admirable. He was trying to be normal as nothing had happened.

I have got my life back now. I just wanted to reach home as soon as possible. I am missing my Naina. My Naina.

When I wrote this, I stopped for a moment, because the way I showed my closeness for her, brought a smile to my face. A sense of infinite peace. I didn't know how I would say sorry to her. I really had no idea but I left this to my heart. I know, within my heart, I have understood everything; I didn't need to spoil my mood. I don't want to sound selfish. But I know, and I am also sure that Naina too understands me.

Epilogue

Next morning, the sky turned saffron with the indescribable hue that heralded the day. The breeze was silently blowing. I just walked towards the window, pulled the curtains aside and opened the window. The warm sunshine splashed over me, cooling me with the breeze. It was very enjoyable and pleasurable on my nerves. The memories of the previous night grew fantastic but then my eyes got stuck on the table.

No diary.

Where is the diary? My eyes skewed, and I rushed towards the table.

I ruffled all the books kept on the table but couldn't see the diary. I checked out my travelling bag, pulled out every single cloth but I couldn't find anything. When I found nothing even in my wardrobe, I grew pensive. I didn't want this diary to fall in anyone's hands. As I was about to walk towards another book shelf, for a moment, I took a glance that flitted like a bird, towards the door. First it didn't get across my mind, but the next moment, I realized someone was there.

I turned around. It was Naina. She was at just outside of the door. I looked at her.

"Naina, so early! What are you doing there? Come inside," I said, smiling. But she didn't reciprocate the same. She walked slowly but didn't sit. I was a bit surprised as her countenance was not normal. I walked towards her. "Is everything okay? And why are you crying?" Dropping my idea to find the diary, I strolled towards her. She kept crying. Tears were endlessly dropping down her face. I sped up to her and raised my eyebrows in a questioning way, and wiped her tears away.

Without uttering any words, she kept staring at me. Her face was no longer radiant. Her eyes, today, was something different. On looking closely at her, I saw that her eyes were red and slightly swollen. It seemed she had been crying for quite some time.

"Hey, what happened? Why are you crying?" I asked.

Without answering my question, she drew her hand from behind. She had my diary in her hand. She handed it over to me.

"Where did you get this?" I asked.

"I am sorry. So sorry," she could speak no further before she broke into tears.

"Sorry?" I was still wondering what's happening.

"I took you diary without your permission yesterday morning," she said. Words were hissing. "Am so sorry, Akshat."

It stunned me and within myself, I was trying to relieve myself. *O god! Hope she didn't read it.* But in some part of my heart, I knew the answer was not in my favour.

"Did you read something?" I asked, looking at her lips, waiting for her to answer "No." but my hope soon crashed when she said, "Yes." And she embraced me tightly and started crying convulsively.

"How did this happen? You never bothered to tell me. Why Akshat?" she asked, still crying.

"I am sorry. I didn't know how to say these things. So, I chose to remain silent," I said, hugging her tight. "I was content to realize you and your feelings...And you were right. Some day someone somewhere will make me realize the meaning of love. I have realized everything."

"Now love is no longer a dream," Naina said and she cuddled in my arms.

RECOMMENDED READING

In Course of True Love!
Sanjeev Ranjan

Take a look at the bittersweet moments of puppy love through the story of the protagonist, Aarush who is a reticent 16-year-old. Things are not going too well in his life – his parents are not impressed with his reasonably good exam score of 90 percent. He subsequently moves to Bokaro to pursue further studies.

There he becomes hopelessly besotted with Aachankya, a girl who happens to be a popular college heartthrob. Surprisingly for him, his feelings are reciprocated too.

But is there more to it than meets the eye? It makes one question whether it is possible for true love to blossom at that tender age or is it just infatuation misconstrued as true love.

ISBN   : 978-93-80349-49-7
Size   : 7.75" x 5.1"
Pages   : 216pp
Binding : PB
Subject : Fiction

Nothing Between Us...
Sanchit Mehrotra

Siddharth fell in love with his childhood friend Avantika, and dreamt of a lovely life together. Everything was working in his favour, before destiny decided against it and intervened. Heart-broken, Siddharth gathers pieces of broken dreams from his soul and comes face to face with Kaya. She loves Siddharth, but cannot fathom a way to resist and overcome the battle between his heart and conscience. Battling the demons of the past, and desperately trying to build up a new relationship with Kaya, Siddharth's trials are never-ending. Will Siddharth be able to move on and make a fresh beginning with Kaya?

ISBN   : 978-93-82665-10-6
Size   : 7.75" x 5.1"
Pages   : 216pp
Binding : PB
Subject : Fiction

RECOMMENDED READING

ISBN : 978-93-82665-05-2
Size : 7.75" x 5.1"
Pages : 212pp
Binding : PB
Subject : Fiction

Romeo, Juliet & Hitler:
Can he put brakes on love
Rohan Gautam

What happens when a girl meets a boy on a train journey and they eventually fall in love? A new Romeo and Juliet are born. And what happens when their families find out? Enter Hitler. Rohan bumps into Shreya perchance and falls in love. As Rohan meanders through his feelings, travels across cities, gets thrown behind bars by pot-bellied policemen, and is almost beaten in his own life and career, he still has to face the biggest test of all – facing Shreya's Hitler brother. Will he be able to win him over? Or will Hitler put brakes on their love?

ISBN : 978-93-82665-06-9
Size : 7.75" x 5.1"
Pages : 312pp
Binding : PB
Subject : Fiction

*Error Code::**Love**:*
Not every story has a hero
Suman Bhattacharya

Kolkata, 2008: Driven by a crazed love, Dev, our next door shy software engineer commits the biggest mistake of his life. Over 72 marathon hours, he loses his education, career, love, and life by a single act of madness.

Bengaluru 2012: Dev reaches Bengaluru in search of a better life. Destiny brings him face to face with his first love once again. He chases the same impossible dream only to find himself burning and failing in love.

The book raises questions allied to grey areas of teen emotions, and lets you find the answers within.